D1490466

The *Note* II

Taking a Chance on Love

ANGELA HUNT

New York Times Best-selling Author

BASED ON THE SCREENPLAY BY DOUGLAS BARR

Tyndale House Publishers, Inc.
Carol Stream, Illinois

Visit Tyndale's exciting Web site at www.tyndale.com

Visit Angela Hunt's Web site at www.angelahuntbooks.com

TYNDALE and Tyndale's quill logo are registered trademarks of Tyndale House Publishers, Inc.

The Note II: Taking a Chance on Love

Copyright © 2009 by National Interfaith Cable Coalition, Inc. All rights reserved.

Cover and interior photographs copyright © 2009 by Brooke Palmer. All rights reserved.

Designed by Beth Sparkman

Edited by Kathryn S. Olson

Published in association with the literary agency of Creative Trust, Inc., 5141 Virginia Way, Suite 320, Brentwood, TN 37027.

Some Scripture quotations are taken from the *Holy Bible*, New Living Translation, copyright © 1996, 2004, 2007 by Tyndale House Foundation. Used by permission of Tyndale House Publishers, Inc., Carol Stream, Illinois 60188. All rights reserved.

Some Scripture quotations are taken from the HOLY BIBLE, NEW INTERNATIONAL VERSION®. NIV®. Copyright © 1973, 1978, 1984 by International Bible Society. Used by permission of Zondervan. All rights reserved.

Library of Congress Cataloging-in-Publication Data

Hunt, Angela Elwell, date.
   The note II : taking a chance on love / Angela Hunt ; based on the screenplay by Douglas Barr.
     p. cm.
   ISBN 978-1-4143-3295-6 (pbk.)
   I. Title.
PS3558.U46747N685 2009
813'.54—dc22   2009005841

Printed in the United States of America

15 14 13 12 11 10 09
 7   6   5   4   3   2   1

FEAR CAN INFECT US EARLY

IN LIFE UNTIL EVENTUALLY IT CUTS

A DEEP GROOVE OF APPREHENSION

IN ALL OUR THINKING.

TO COUNTERACT IT, LET FAITH,

HOPE, AND COURAGE

ENTER YOUR THINKING.

FEAR IS STRONG,

BUT FAITH IS STRONGER YET.

—NORMAN VINCENT PEALE

One

WITH ONE ELBOW propped on her desk, Peyton MacGruder chewed on the edge of a fingernail and glared at the clock on the wall. On days like this, when she was twenty minutes away from her deadline and far from finished with her column, she could swear that the minute hand swept over the clock face at double speed.

She transferred her gaze to the computer monitor and fluttered her fingers over the keyboard. Some days the magic worked and the words flowed. Other days she might as well be typing gibberish.

She skimmed the half-completed column on her screen and tried to focus her thoughts. Last week a reader had written that she was afraid to trust a brother-in-law who had stolen from her in the past. Peyton had answered that forgiveness was important, but experience could not be ignored. And when it came to matters of the heart, caution should always trump passion. Dozens of readers had e-mailed, filling her in-box with responses, most of them supportive.

Now she was working on a recap that included reader comments, but everything she'd written so far looked like extended self-congratulation. She needed a corroborating opinion . . . and *any* column could be improved with an appropriate quote, couldn't it? She reached for her dictionary of popular quotations, scanned the index, and jabbed her finger at an appropriate entry. Smiling with satisfaction, she propped her reading glasses on the end of her nose and worked the quote into her piece:

> *And so, dear readers, when it comes to dealing with relationships, perhaps we should keep the words of Eumenides in mind. That venerable sage once wrote, "There are times when fear is good. It must keep its watchful place at the heart's controls. There is advantage in the wisdom won from pain."*
> *Perhaps a happy heart is, at its core, a cautious heart.*

There. She leaned back and clicked the word count tool. Seven hundred words—not bad. The dragon lady shouldn't have to cut any of this column.

After a quick proofread, Peyton clicked Send and addressed the file to Nora Chilton, senior features editor. Another click and away it went.

She turned as something slapped the surface of her desk. Mandi Hillridge, an overenthusiastic intern from the University of North Carolina Wilmington, stood in the aisle, her arms filled with folders. Peyton picked up the envelope Mandi had tossed her way and studied the return address. "Am I supposed to know this Eve Miller?"

Mandi shifted her burden from one arm to the other. "I doubt it. I think she's a reader."

Peyton ran her fingertip across the ragged edge. "Why has this letter been opened?"

"Because Phil Brinker didn't check the address before he tore into it. Our stellar mailroom staff mistakenly delivered it to him while he was in New York working on that story about the media covering the media. He just got back and told me to bring it to you." Mandi stepped closer, her eyes gleaming. "You want me to go fuss at the guys in the mailroom? One of them's kinda cute."

Peyton glanced over the short walls of the reporters' cubicles and saw Nora stepping out of the elevator. "No." She propped both elbows up on her desk. "I want you to get me two Tylenol. Extra strength."

"You have a headache?"

"Not yet."

Mandi turned in time to see Nora approaching, a folded newspaper in hand. Even from her desk Peyton recognized the distinctive banner that contained her byline and staff photo. Had Nora come down to complain about a column that had already run? She wouldn't, unless one of the higher-ups sent her to confront Peyton about some obscure point.

"About that headache—" Mandi lowered her voice—"I'll bring the bottle."

The young woman hurried away as Nora approached Peyton's desk. The editor waved the paper before Peyton's anxious gaze and nodded. "By the way, about this column last week? You were absolutely right."

"That's a nice change." Peyton managed a smile. "About what?"

"Passion. It should always be tempered with caution. Especially when it comes to affairs of the heart."

Peyton straightened in her chair, not certain why the editor had felt compelled to personally deliver this bit of elaboration. "You speaking from conviction or firsthand experience?"

Nora managed a coy smile. "None of your business. Anyway, you've been doing really good work lately. I had my doubts at first, but you've grown into the job."

"You came all the way down here to pat me on the back?"

"Actually, I came down here to tell you that in addition to writing the Heart Healer, I'm going to need you to handle a feature or two for the Lifestyles section. We got the call last night; Marlo Evans had a baby boy, so she'll be out on maternity leave for the next several weeks."

Peyton dropped her head to her hand and groaned. "Why not use freelancers?"

"Because I don't have the patience or the finances to deal with neophytes. The budget cuts have made it necessary for all of us to pick up the slack now and then. Besides—" her mouth curved in a wry smile—"you're fast and you're good at researching. A feature or two shouldn't be a problem for you."

"But I'm swamped with—" Peyton swallowed the rest of her complaint as sports editor King Danville moved into her line of vision. A warm feeling settled in the pit of her stomach and brought a smile to her lips. Would she ever stop feeling all gushy and girly whenever King approached her desk?

King glanced at the features editor before returning Peyton's smile. "Hello, Nora."

Nora's chin dipped in a stiff nod. "Kingston."

Like a flower seeking the sun, Peyton shifted to face the man who had recently brought new joy to her life. "I was just telling Nora that these days I don't have time to keep up with my column *and* write a weekly feature, no matter how occasional it is."

Nora glanced from Peyton to King and then arched a brow. "Perhaps if you temper your newfound passion, you'll find the time."

King grinned as the editor smiled and moved toward the elevator; then he pulled a white bottle from his jacket pocket and shook it. Peyton placed the familiar rattle within seconds: Extra Strength Tylenol, as requested.

"Ran into Mandi in the coffee room," King explained. "She said you were going to need these."

"She was right." Peyton sighed. "Nora seems to think I can sit down and whip up a decent feature while I'm outlining my next column. I don't know where she got the idea that I'm some kind of writing machine."

"Maybe from the fact that you write so fast you make the rest of us look like we're moving backward."

Peyton shook her head, unwilling to accept praise she didn't deserve. She knew the truth—she could turn an assignment around quickly because outside the newspaper office she had no life. While other writers struggled to work amid the pressures of family schedules, children's homework, school events, sporting activities, and the needs of a spouse, Peyton only had to take care of herself and her two cats.

At least that's the way things were before King and Christine came into her life. The situation was a little different now, and she was feeling the pressure.

"I'm not that fast," she insisted. "And I'm not that versatile."

"Then don't cave so quickly, MacGruder. Just because Nora's your boss doesn't mean you have to let her push you around."

"I was ready to push back until she played the guilt card. When she mentioned the budget cuts, I realized how lucky I am to even be employed. How can I not agree to write whatever she wants?"

"That's what I like about you—you're a solid team player."

"I'm a pushover."

King smiled and stepped to the side of Peyton's desk. "In that case, I'd better prescribe two of these—" he held up the bottle of pain relievers—"or one of these." Before Peyton could point out that they were surrounded by coworkers in cubicles, he bent and pressed a kiss to her lips. She closed her eyes, ready to forget about an audience of staff reporters, clerks, and copy editors, but the kiss didn't last.

She looked up at him, unsatisfied.

"Do any good?" he asked.

"Not sure. Try again. Maybe increase the dosage."

He bent, his lips warming hers with more passion this time. When he finally pulled away, Peyton exhaled a long sigh of happiness . . . and the writers around her erupted into applause.

Peyton grinned as her cheeks warmed. "They approve."

"I don't give a fig about them. What did you think?"

"Um . . . better."

"Only *better*? Well, you know what they say about practice making perfect . . ."

As the other reporters hooted and King leaned in for yet another kiss, Peyton pressed her palm against the center of his chest. "You know, it's this kind of temptation that led to Marlo Evans's maternity leave. And, in turn, to my impending headache. So maybe we should get back to work."

With a roguish grin, King straightened and stepped away from her chair. "Yes, ma'am."

"But after work—" Peyton squinted at him—"would you want to go for a jog with me and Christine? We wanted to run the paths down by the shoreline."

King shook his head. "Enticing offer, but I've got to run out to the university after I finish up today. David needs to talk to me about something. He says it's important."

Peyton nodded, once again reminded that their relationship was not as simple as it would have been if they'd met in their twenties. She had Christine to consider, and King had David. Both children, hers and his, were nearly grown, and both had been forced to deal with the aftermath of their parents' unwise decisions.

"MacGruder." King's voice, warm and insistent, drew her from her thoughts. "Maybe I'll stop by your place later."

"I'd like that." Peyton offered him a forgiving smile. "I'll be waiting."

King took two steps toward his office, then halted. "Hey—" he turned, propping his arms on the cubicle wall—"I found an interesting e-mail in my in-box this morning. A friend in New

York said my name recently came up in a board meeting at the *Times*."

Peyton felt a frigid finger touch the base of her spine. "The *New York Times?*"

He chuckled. "Hard to imagine, huh? Moving from the *Middleborough Times* to the Gray Lady?"

"Your name came up in a board meeting? What does that mean, exactly?"

He shrugged. "I don't know, but I'll keep you posted."

As he walked away, exchanging gibes with other writers as he passed their desks, Peyton felt fear blow down the back of her neck. Any other journalist would be salivating at the thought of writing for the *Times*, but King never seemed to get ahead of himself. Contentment was one of his primary virtues, and Peyton hadn't realized how much she'd been counting on his ability to remain satisfied with the status quo.

What would she do if she lost him?

The thought struck like a blow to the chest, stealing her breath. Until recently, she had managed to keep herself detached from complicated personal relationships. But then the tragedy of a horrific plane crash taught her about the brevity of life and the importance of connection. Now she was desperate to understand two precious people, but understanding took time, and time was something she no longer possessed in abundance.

She forced herself to take a deep breath and steady her pulse. No one was abandoning her; the world had not shifted on its axis.

Her imagination was simply working overtime, a tendency that nearly always resulted in needless worry and borrowed trouble.

With her gift for imagining disaster, maybe she should have been a novelist.

When she swiveled toward her computer, determined to set her fears aside and tackle her e-mail, her gaze fell again on the envelope from Eve Miller. The postmark was five days in the past, so by now the woman's comments were old news. And in an electronic society, old news was dead news.

Peyton tossed the envelope into a bin filled with unopened letters and turned her attention to her in-box.

Peyton slid behind the wheel of her car, tossed her purse into the empty passenger seat, and fumbled with the buckle of her seat belt. When she was certain the car's computer wouldn't scold her for forgetting some vital procedure, she turned the ignition switch and waited for the automatic seat to slide forward, tilt, rise, and whatever else it did to adjust to her frame.

King had talked her into buying this vehicle last weekend, insisting that her old car was only a few miles away from imploding. "Ninety-eight thousand miles?" he exclaimed after glimpsing her odometer. "Good grief, MacGruder, are you going for some kind of endurance record?"

She had to admit the new vehicle was nice, but its myriad bells and whistles bewildered her. She hadn't taken the time to read the manual, and she barely managed to sit through the salesman's demonstration. "I don't have time to fuss with fancy gadgets," she told the desperate young man who had greeted her and King at the auto dealership. "So just point me toward something safe and inexpensive. Something I won't have to give up chocolate to afford."

Like a village matchmaker, the salesman grinned and fixed her up with this sleek blue machine, which he kept calling a crossover—a cross between a sedan and an SUV. She had a feeling the vehicle was too big to be economical or politically correct, but since an entire row of similar vehicles waited behind a fence at the dealership, the manager was probably eager to move his inventory. Regardless, the car earned good crash ratings, it used less gasoline than a tank, *and* it had the one accessory she couldn't live without: a CD player.

Before putting the car in gear, Peyton punched the button of the stereo system and relaxed when the professional reader's voice poured through the surround sound speakers. She'd bought this audiobook about mothers and daughters shortly after telling Christine the truth about their relationship—yes, they were reporter and reader, but they were also biological mother and daughter. Eighteen years and difficult circumstances had kept them apart, but a series of newspaper columns had brought them back together.

Now Peyton wanted nothing more than to be the mother she would have been if tragedy hadn't intervened. A heaven-sent miracle had restored the child she'd been forced to surrender for adoption, and Peyton didn't want to forfeit this second chance to love. And parent. And occasionally nag.

She and Christine were still in the midst of that awkward

getting-to-know-you phase, but Peyton felt they'd made great strides in their relationship. They tried to talk every day, even if only briefly, and though Christine still lived in the house she'd inherited from her adoptive parents, she felt free enough to drop into Peyton's home unannounced, as any daughter naturally would.

Still, Christine rarely called Peyton "Mom." When necessary, she called Peyton by name . . . or she didn't call her anything at all.

"By late adolescence," a confident voice intoned as Peyton put the car in gear and backed out of the parking space, "most daughters can be placed in one of three categories—distant, dissatisfied, or dependent. Do any of these words remind you of the young woman in your life?"

Peyton shook her head and shifted into drive. The author needed a fourth category for Christine—maybe *delightful*. They were still in the honeymoon phase, each of them unbearably grateful to have found the other. They might have disagreements later—in fact, they probably would—but for now Peyton was thrilled to be able to know and love the young woman who had never been far from her thoughts and prayers.

"Outstanding mothers devote most of their time to their children, instilling healthy values into daughters who will become outstanding mothers themselves," the reader continued, "but unsuitable mothers abandon and abuse."

Peyton winced at the author's use of the word *abandon*.

"Bottom line, if you provide your child with what she needs—clothing, shelter, food, affection—you, concerned mother, are off the hook if your daughter makes unwise decisions. After you have taught your child right from wrong, your daughter has the freedom to choose . . . right *or* wrong. Do not blame yourself if she chooses to learn life's lessons through negative experiences."

Peyton frowned as she pulled out of the parking lot and into traffic. Over the years, she'd covered dozens of stories involving teenage delinquents—wayward boys who got mixed up with guns and drugs, runaway girls who ended up on the street or in the hospital because they went looking for love in all the wrong faces. Behind every sad teenager's story, Peyton found a distraught mother who couldn't seem to understand how her child ended up in such a deplorable state.

She hated to admit it, but every time she interviewed one of those mothers, she'd walked away feeling resentful and slightly smug, convinced that she would have managed better if only given a chance. But now that she *was* being given an opportunity to mother a teen, she had no idea what she was supposed to do.

To make matters worse, her time of greatest influence would be limited. After the plane crash in which her father died, Christine had taken time off to grieve, but soon she'd go back to school and get busy with her studies. She'd probably meet a young man on campus and want to settle down. Then she'd center her world on her husband and her children, and she'd expect Peyton to focus on being a doting grandmother, not a mom. So this precious opportunity to parent her daughter would be relatively short-lived.

Peyton pulled up to the red light at an intersection and

snapped off the CD player. The bookstores were loaded with books about how to parent newborns, toddlers, middle schoolers, and teens, but no one had much advice for brand-new parents of young adults.

No one even seemed to be able to answer Peyton's most basic question—at eighteen, which did Christine need most: an authority figure or a friend?

Two

PEYTON PULLED INTO the parking lot outside the Vintage Groove, a shop that sold old record albums and movie posters, and spotted her daughter standing near the store window. Beneath her dark hair, the girl's cheeks were rosy and her eyes sparkled when she smiled in answer to Peyton's wave. For an instant she looked so much like Gil that Peyton caught her breath. If only he could see her now . . .

She blinked the images of the past away, then motioned Christine forward and bent to look for the button that would unlock the passenger door. One of these days she'd know the purpose of all the controls on the driver's armrest.

She watched as her daughter approached the car and couldn't help but notice that the tattooed man behind the counter watched Christine, too. Who was he, and why was he so interested in a woman who was much too young for him?

"Hey." Christine moved Peyton's purse onto her lap as she climbed into the car. "Ready to run?"

"Ready as I'll ever be." Peyton slid the car into reverse and glanced over her shoulder. "Did you have a nice day?"

Christine made a face. "So-so. Nothing great, nothing too bad."

Peyton put the car in drive. "Same here. Except that Nora announced that she's going to be handing out extra assignments in the coming weeks. One of our writers went out on maternity leave."

Christine blinked. "Does that mean we can't spend as much time—"

"Not at all." Peyton reached over and patted the girl's hand. "Don't you worry. I'll squeeze in the extra work somewhere. Nothing's going to interfere with our time together."

She pulled out into traffic and headed toward the highway that would take them to the North Carolina shoreline. This stretch of asphalt ran straight from the heart of Middleborough to the beach, and every time Peyton drove it, she couldn't help but think of the horrible day when PanWorld Flight 848 went down in the bay. That tragedy claimed the life of 261 crew and passengers, among them Christine's adoptive father.

That sad fact stood in front of Peyton's happiness, reminding her to temper the joy she felt in finding her daughter. She couldn't allow herself to forget that three months ago Christine had lost her single surviving adoptive parent, the only father she would ever know. Peyton didn't want the girl to feel that she walked a tightrope, struggling to balance her affection between different sets of parents, those who gave her life and those who gave her *a* life.

"So—" Peyton kept her gaze on the road and gripped the steering wheel—"tell me a little something about this boyfriend of yours."

Christine snorted. "What boyfriend?"

"You know who I mean. Mr. Body Art, the guy who works with you. I saw him staring at you when I looked through the store window."

Christine made a face. "Mike? He's not my boyfriend."

"Does he know that? He looked awfully interested to me."

"He's just a friend."

"The kind with benefits?"

Christine laughed. "Did you read about that in *Ladies' Home Journal* or something?"

"You think I'm too much of a nerd to know what's going on out there?"

"I don't think you're a nerd. But you're not exactly . . ."

"What?"

"Never mind. You're fine just the way you are."

I wish. Peyton braked and flipped her signal for a left turn into the parking lot. How should she say what must be said next? She wanted to share her values with Christine, but she didn't want to come across as preachy or prudish. But *someone* had to counter all the hedonistic messages being trumpeted on television and in the movies. Wasn't that part of a mother's job?

She inhaled a deep breath. "You know sex is a sacred and private thing, right?"

Christine giggled and turned away. "Oh, puh-lease. Tell me we're not having this conversation now."

Peyton bit her lip. What did *that* mean? Did Christine not want to ever talk about this kind of thing? Where was the line between being too disinterested and being too nosy? If Peyton inadvertently crossed the line, would Christine throw her hands up and decide this relationship wasn't worth the trouble?

"I'm just saying that you need to guard your heart and be cautious in love." Peyton forced a smile as she turned into the lot. "I suppose you think your relationships are none of my business."

Christine's head turned. "Of course they're your business. You're my mother."

"Can't tell you how weird that still sounds." The words slipped out before Peyton could stop them and seemed to hang in the car as she pulled into an empty parking space. Only after killing the engine did she realize that her daughter was staring at her. "What's wrong?"

"What do you mean?" Christine asked, her voice slow and hesitant. "What's weird about it?"

Apparently she had touched a sensitive spot. "I didn't mean anything negative," Peyton hurried to explain. "But you have to realize, I never had a chance to mother you before my father and the psychiatrist talked me into agreeing to an adoption plan for you. I didn't even want to see you; I couldn't bear the pain of knowing what I'd almost done when I tried to take my life. I've come a long way since those days, but after so many years of living alone, I'm a long way from knowing how to be a decent mother. I'm certainly willing to learn, though."

Christine wiped away a tear and offered a shy smile. "How about I give you some advice?"

"Happy to hear it."

"First of all," she began, "I'm eighteen, so I don't need a smother mother or a helicopter parent." Her face reddened as emotions rose from somewhere deep inside. "But don't think I don't want you around. I'll never get tired of hearing that you'll never leave me again, so you can keep on reminding me. I don't want to lose you, not for any reason. Not ever!"

Peyton winced at the sound of insecurity and longing in Christine's voice. Reaching across the space between them, she wrapped her arms around her daughter and held her tight, rubbing her back as she murmured all the soothing things she would have said if they had known each other for years instead of weeks. "Don't worry, baby," she finished, her own throat clotting with emotion. "Now that I've found you, you're stuck with me for good."

Christine hiccuped a sob, but she was smiling when she pulled away. "Let's go—" she swiped at her wet cheeks—"before this morphs into a total tearfest."

Peyton stepped out of the car, stashed her purse in the cargo area, and inhaled the scents of low tide and sea salt before pressing the autolock on the remote. When the vehicle chirped in reply, she braced her foot on the bumper and attempted to touch her toes.

"King says we should always stretch before we run," she said, hoping Christine wouldn't burst into laughter at the sight of her feeble efforts.

"He would know." Christine propped her sneakered foot on the bumper and bent her forehead to her left knee without straining.

Peyton straightened and sighed at the sight of her dark-haired daughter against the striking vista of blue sky and ocean. Oh, to be young, flexible, and blissfully unaware of the aches and pains to come.

When Christine lowered her left leg in order to stretch her right, Peyton tiptoed toward another sensitive subject. "So . . . how are you coping these days? Still having bad dreams about your dad? the crash?"

Christine straightened. "Not so often. I actually started cleaning out Dad's closet the other day. Packing up his stuff."

"Really? That's a big step."

"Yeah. I didn't get too far with it, though. I found a box of letters he wrote to Mom while he was in the service, and I stopped to read a couple of them. After that, I was such a mess I didn't know what to do. How do you throw something like that away? How could I throw any of his stuff away? I had to quit and walk out of the room."

Peyton cast about for the right words. This sort of conversation might come naturally for other mothers, but she had always been better at asking questions than delivering answers.

"It *is* hard," she finally ventured. "I couldn't face that job for a long time after Gil . . . after your father died. I did feel better, though, once I got it done. It felt like I'd crossed a bridge or something and left some of the resentment and depression behind." She hesitated. "Of course, this was months after the accident and a while after you were born." *And while I was still under my psychiatrist's care. Even he couldn't help me get over the guilt of losing you.*

"I don't know." Christine's gaze swept the watery horizon, her eyes unfocused and distant. "I guess I should give it another try."

Peyton stepped closer. "How about I stop by Saturday morning? I could give you a hand."

Christine met Peyton's gaze. After a moment's hesitation, she nodded. "Okay. I've actually been thinking a lot about my future. Packing up the past might be a good way to jump-start things."

Peyton slipped her arm through her daughter's. "That's the spirit. Now—I'll race you to the first bench and back. Just be careful not to leave me in the dust, okay? I might choke."

Christine laughed. "I won't leave you anywhere. Not for any reason."

৵

The roommate's abrupt departure, King realized, should have been a warning. He had no sooner knocked on the door and said, "David? It's Dad," when the door opened and Brian or Ryan or whatever his name was slipped out with only a quick "How are ya?" in greeting.

King took advantage of the open door and stepped into the room. Two twin beds, two desks, and two dressers filled the small space, but dirty clothes, pizza boxes, and soft drink cans littered every horizontal surface. The room smelled of stale pizza and sweat, scents that carried King back to his own days in the dorm. A tangle of earbuds and cords cluttered David's desk, most of them spiderwebbed over four unopened cans of Red Bull and a laptop.

His son, a college sophomore, sat on the edge of his bed, his eyes puffy and a muscle clenched along his jaw. "Hey," David said, his voice gruff. "Sorry, I was asleep."

King bit back a remark about sleeping through afternoon classes. He had to trust David to manage his own schedule. "You wanted to talk to me about something?"

"Yeah." David lifted his chin and braced his shoulders. "It's about baseball."

"The coach not playing you enough?"

"Forget about the coach, Dad; this is about me and baseball. I quit the team."

For an instant, King was certain David was pulling his leg, maybe trying to distract him with a weak joke. But the boy's eyes were serious, and the customary curve of good humor was missing from his mouth.

King stared at his son and sank to the edge of a chair draped with stained T-shirts. "I don't get it; how can you quit the team? Baseball's been your life since the first time you whacked a T-ball."

David gripped the edge of his mattress. "Well . . . it's not anymore, okay? Look, Dad, I'm late for class." He rose and moved toward the doorway, probably thinking he could slide out of the room before King caught him. But his old man hadn't petrified yet.

"Hold on, Son." King stood and caught the edge of the door before David could slip away. "We're not done here."

David turned, rolling his eyes. Sensing that it wouldn't be good to vent his frustration here in the dorm, King took a deep breath and struggled to maintain control of his temper. "Son, I—"

"Yeah?" Bitterness dripped from the word.

"I just hate to see you give it up, that's all. I mean, you have a real talent for the game."

"Spare me."

"What do you mean?"

David shook his head. "I have decent stuff, but my fastball stinks. You and I both know that."

King smiled. "Ease up, kid. Your body won't be fully mature until you're twenty-five. Realistically, right now you can't know what you have and what you don't have."

"What I *don't* have is any fire on my fastball or in my gut for baseball, not anymore. Okay? So can we just drop it?"

King tried another approach. "What about your scholarship?"

David shot him a twisted smile. "Obviously, if I don't play, I don't get a free ride."

King exhaled slowly through his teeth. What *was* it with kids today? Did they really think their parents had money trees growing in the backyard?

"What?" A tense note underlined David's voice as his eyes read the exasperation on King's face. "You won't cover me?"

"I didn't say that."

David snorted. "Hey, you know what? Don't worry about it."

He moved forward again, but King kept his arm locked and his hand on the door. "What's that supposed to mean?"

"It means—" David gripped the door handle and pulled,

surprising King with his strength—"don't worry about me. I'll stay out of your hair."

With that he slipped through the doorway and jogged down the hall, the angry slap of his sneakers echoing in the tiled corridor.

King gritted his teeth and glanced around the messy dorm room, his gaze finally landing on a photograph stuck into the mirror frame. The picture featured him and David standing in a river, each of them holding a line filled with several good-size trout.

Once upon a time, David had been a big-eyed, adorable, compliant child. Once upon a time, they had been buddies. Where had the years gone, and what had happened to change things?

After a low-calorie frozen dinner, Peyton snuggled into the sofa, a wool wrap around her shoulders and a laptop in her lap. By the light of the flickering fireplace, she typed out preliminary summaries for the columns she would need to write this month and then made a few notes for a proposed feature article on parenting older adolescents. If Nora really wanted her to write a feature, she might as well get some use out of the books she'd been reading about mother-daughter relationships.

Finally she compiled her notes into a memo for the features editor. Nora ought to be pleased—but she'd probably just nod as if she expected no less from one of her "team players."

Peyton glanced at the clock on the mantel. Eight o'clock and not a word from King. His meeting with David must have gone well; perhaps they went out to dinner. King's favorite barbecue place had an all-you-can-eat platter guaranteed to satisfy even the hungriest adolescent.

She might as well catch up on her correspondence. Her four-times weekly column generated hundreds of e-mails, most of which were easy to acknowledge. Many of Peyton's correspondents were eager to report that they'd been touched by a story or found her information useful, though occasionally she received letters from people who took her to task for some ill-considered word or a particular point of view. Though she tried to avoid the topics of politics and religion—best to leave those powder kegs for the editorial pages—every once in a while she wrote up a story that couldn't be told without mentioning God or government. After those columns ran, Peyton's in-box invariably sizzled with heated opinions.

After typing dozens of "Thanks, good to hear from you" responses, she clicked Send on the last e-mail and glanced at the bag resting by the side of the sofa. She'd dropped a handful of regular correspondence into it on her way out of the office, and now a letter jutted toward her, an envelope addressed in the elegant but spidery handwriting of an older woman.

A woman obviously not comfortable with the informality of e-mail . . . Mrs. Eve Miller.

Sighing, Peyton pulled the envelope from her bag and slid the letter from the envelope. A moment later, she looked up as her doorbell rang. She dropped the page onto the sofa, crossed to the foyer in sock-clad feet, and peered through the sidelights at a familiar figure. King.

Immediately her spirits lifted.

"I'd almost given up on you," she said, opening the door.

His mouth curled in a one-sided smile. "You wouldn't do that, would you?"

"I wouldn't want to." She tipped her head back as he stepped into the circle of her arms and kissed her—for real this time, for there were no coworkers, no prowling editors, no googly-eyed interns spying from behind cubicle walls.

After a long moment, King lifted his head. "Now that's what I call a welcome, MacGruder."

"My pleasure." She took his hand and led him into the living room. "Come sit with me. And tell me what David had to say. What's the boy up to?"

King groaned as he dropped onto the sofa. "He's quitting baseball."

"You're kidding. Did he say why?"

"Just that he's burned out. At twenty, the kid thinks he's a has-been."

Peyton sat sideways on the sofa and tucked her cold toes beneath a seat cushion. "I can't believe it."

"Yeah. Well, go figure. Who knows what kids are thinking these days?"

Peyton cast about for some wise or witty bit of parenting advice and came up empty. "Well . . . what are you going to do?"

"I'm going to talk to him again. And again, if necessary. I can't just let him throw his talent away."

She smiled. "Do you want anything? food? drink?"

"Just you. Come here." He gestured to her, the warmth of affection sparkling in his eyes, and Peyton forgot all about the correspondence scattered over her sofa. She leaned forward and let him draw her into his arms; then she heard the crunch of paper as her knee mangled Eve Miller's letter.

King peered down at the crumpled page. "What's that?"

"Oh, nothing important, just a reader letter."

"Fan mail?" Grinning, he pulled the page free. "You shouldn't be so careless with fan letters, MacGruder. I keep all mine in a special file. Both of them."

She rolled her eyes and settled into the cozy space beneath his arm. "This isn't exactly a fan letter. This woman stopped just short of calling one of my columns inane."

"Is she a crackpot?"

Peyton tilted her head and studied the delicate handwriting. "I don't think so. Actually, I'm a little intrigued by her comments. I think—"

"Do you mind?" King pulled his reading glasses from his pocket and began to read the letter aloud: "'Dear Heart Healer: I'm an avid reader of your column. A fan, if you will, and as such I feel it's my duty to tell you when you're full of baloney.'" He barked a laugh. "Ouch."

Peyton shrugged. "See what I mean?"

King kept reading: "'I can assure you, your readers take your words very seriously, so when you tell them to "let caution trump passion," you do them a grave disservice. I know this from painful experience, as I followed similar counsel nearly forty years ago and regret my actions to this day. Perhaps we might discuss the appropriate time to "take a chance on love" over a cup of tea. And while doing so, I'm quite sure I'll be able to dissuade you of your misguided opinion. If you're willing, kindly reach me at the number below. Sincerely, Eve Miller.'"

King lowered the letter. "So . . . are you going to call her?"

"You think I should? I've already done a follow-up on the column that set her off."

He shrugged. "Give her a call; see what her story is. Who knows? You might get a column out of it. And maybe . . ."

"Maybe what?"

King looked as though he might say something else; then he clamped his mouth shut and smiled. "Nothing."

"What?" Peyton pulled away to better look at him. "You think I'm full of baloney, too, don't you?"

"I didn't say that."

"You'd better be careful, big guy. I get enough snide comments from Nora. But for the record, she agrees with me on this one. She actually stopped by to give me a compliment today."

"Nervous Nora? She must have had ulterior motives."

"Well—" Peyton felt her mouth twist—"you know she asked me to write an extra feature this month. But she still agrees that caution should temper passion."

A grin overtook King's features. "How did the wise man put it? To everything there is a season—a time to be cautious, and a time to run with your impulse."

"I don't think that's exactly what Solomon said, but I get your point." Peyton rose up and kissed King's cheek. He still smelled faintly of cologne, and his skin felt warm beneath her lips.

"Like I said—" his arm tightened around her shoulder— "there's a time to be restrained . . ."

She leaned over and kissed his other cheek. "And . . . ?"

"And a time to celebrate being alone . . . together."

"You're a bit of a wise man yourself." She kissed the tip of his nose and lowered her forehead to his. "What time would you say it is now?"

He pulled her into his arms. If he had an answer, she never heard it.

Three

THE NEXT MORNING, Peyton stepped off the elevator and spotted Mandi waiting in the foyer, a steaming cup of coffee in her hand. "Like a beacon in a storm, Mandi, you are a lifesaver!" She took the cup and sipped from it without slowing her stride.

Like a dutiful puppy, Mandi followed her through the maze of cubicles. "Good morning, but you're already behind schedule. Up late last night?"

Peyton turned and pointed to the shadowed half circles beneath her eyes. "Late enough to need a bellhop for these bags."

"Okay, then. You have a news budget meeting in five minutes, conference room. Nora's already called. She wants nut grafs on your upcoming columns ASAP. And she wants to talk to you about the feature for this month."

Peyton dropped her bag on her desk and pulled Eve's letter from a compartment. "Understood. Do me a favor, will you? Tell Nora I'm on my way—" she handed the envelope to her intern—"and see if you can reach this woman."

Mandi glanced at the return address. "Wasn't this the lost letter?"

"Right. Anyway, when you get ahold of Mrs. Miller, tell her I'd like to take her up on her offer."

"She's selling something?"

"Read the letter and you'll understand." Peyton dropped into her chair and picked up the phone. "Now, I'm going to check in with my daughter for a minute; then I'll head to the conference room. Thanks, Mandi. And by the way—" she pointed at Mandi's skirt and sweater—"nice outfit. Very professional."

While the intern sailed away to her own desk, Peyton dialed Christine's cell phone, then settled back and waited for the sound of the girl's welcoming voice. She had no deadline today, which meant she might be able to slip out at lunchtime and meet Christine at a local restaurant.

Her heart warmed at the prospect of telling anyone who asked that she was *taking her daughter to lunch*. After all they'd been through, she would never take that pleasure for granted.

Peyton slipped into the conference room and hoped no one would notice that she was twenty minutes late. Most everyone in the room was focused on Nora, who stood before the whiteboard, reading from a subscriber letter.

Peyton flashed a smile at Chandra Thomas, the woman nearest the only empty chair. Chandra, a part-timer who wrote a weekly column called the Pet Vet, nodded without smiling, apparently intent upon whatever Nora was reading.

Peyton settled into the empty seat and pulled out her steno pad, ready to jot down any notes that might be important. She fixed her face into serious lines, the picture of a dedicated reporter, and then she felt King's gaze.

She shifted and found him sitting near the head of the table, to Nora's left. He winked when he caught her eye, and her face warmed in response. She shook her head, aware that several others were twittering, but reassumed her poker face when Nora peered over the top of her reading glasses to see what had caused the ripple of inattention.

"As you can see—" the editor lowered the letter in her hand—"your words *do* make a profound difference in readers' lives. Don't forget the special editions coming up this month, get nut grafs to your department editors ASAP, and, Peyton MacGruder—glad you could join us this morning. Be sure to see me before you go."

As the meeting broke up, Chandra leaned toward Peyton, a twinkle in her eye. "Sounds like you're in for it this time."

Peyton chuffed. "What'd I do?"

"She told us, but I'm not going to steal Nora's thunder." Chandra grinned and stood, then pointed her pencil in Peyton's direction. "By the way, MacGruder, do you know anyone who wants a Great Dane? I heard about a big boy in rescue who needs a new home."

Peyton shivered. "I'm a cat person. Besides, what family in their right mind would want one of those monsters in the house?"

"Lots of families I know. I'd keep this one, but I already

have two Danes. The bedroom's getting a little crowded." She glanced across the room. "Hey, Kingston, how do you feel about Marmaduke?"

Peyton grimaced, hoping that King wouldn't be persuaded by Chandra's appeal. She would have stood and waved for his attention, but Nora had worked her way through the crowd.

"Peyton." The editor sat on the edge of the conference table. "First of all, let me be the first to offer my congratulations."

"Um, thanks." Peyton managed a tentative smile. "What for?"

"If you'd come in on time, you'd already know. As of March 15, you will have been the paper's Heart Healer for one year. As I mentioned the other day, I had my doubts about you at first, but you've turned that column around and made it your own. Well done."

Peyton blinked as King walked up, clapping. "The applause was a lot louder when she told the group." He grinned, his eyes sparkling with more than a hint of flirtation. "Too bad you weren't here to appreciate it."

Peyton arched a brow. She'd been late to the meeting because she got a late start this morning; she got a late start because a gentleman caller had stayed late last night. And King knew very well who *that* was.

"In any case," Nora continued, her tone dry, "since your column is one of our most popular, I think it'd be good to commemorate the anniversary. I'd like you to write a special feature for the March 15 weekend edition—maybe 'Life Lessons I've Learned as the Heart Healer.' Okay, that's wordy, but feel free to tighten it up."

Peyton stared, her mind spinning with bewilderment. "You want me to *what*?"

"Write a summation of your first year as a columnist. I'm thinking two thousand words, due to me by the fourteenth. We'll give you space above the fold of the Lifestyles section, plus a banner ad on the front page."

"Whoo-hoo." King lifted both brows. "Way to go, MacGruder."

She frowned. "You didn't take that dog, did you?"

"What dog—oh, Chandra's? No, don't worry. But hey—an anniversary! That's great news."

Peyton shifted her gaze back to Nora. "Lessons I've learned? But what if I—"

"Oh." The editor held up a finger. "I almost forgot. Ed Carson of the Creator's Syndicate called me last week and asked about you. They won't even consider a columnist who's been on the job less than a year, but he'd like to see some of your clips. You should send him the feature after it runs."

Peyton nodded in an attempt to cover her confusion. Syndication was every columnist's dream, and she'd actually signed a contract with Howard Features when her column received national attention after the tragedy of PanWorld 848. But the syndicate had pressed for exclusives she hadn't been willing to give, so they agreed to terminate their agreement after only a few weeks.

But here she was, again looking at an opportunity to take her column nationwide. Syndication meant an increased readership, a substantial salary, job security, and a measure of fame. Syndication meant her name would be as familiar as Dave Barry's,

Maureen Dowd's, and Ellen Goodman's. Syndication meant success.

All she had to do was figure out what life lessons she had learned as the Heart Healer.

With the phone clamped between her shoulder and her ear, Peyton dabbed at her cheeks with a makeup brush and frowned at her mirror. Applying color while on the phone put a woman at a distinct disadvantage; if she wasn't careful, one cheek was going to be pinker than the other.

"What do you mean, 'no luck'?" she asked Mandi, who had called from the office in a minor panic. "How many times did you try Eve Miller?"

"About a zillion," Mandi answered. "I called at least once every hour, and I kept calling all day."

"No answering machine?"

"Nada. The phone just kept ringing."

Peyton sighed, then heard the faint beep of her security system. King must have arrived; she told him to let himself in if she didn't answer the doorbell. An instant later, she heard his voice from the foyer: "Man on the floor!"

"Hang on!" she called back, covering the phone. "I'm running late, as usual."

She sat on the edge of the bed, focusing her attention on Mandi. "Okay, then, so we won't be going with *that* column tomorrow. I'll come up with something generic, but I don't want to let this woman slip through the cracks. Tomorrow morning, call Mrs. Miller again. Try her number a zillion and one times, okay?"

"You got it. Have a good time tonight."

"We plan to. Thanks, Mandi."

Peyton clicked off the phone and tossed it on the bed, then reached for her earrings on the bureau. "Be down in a second," she called toward the hallway. "Help yourself to something from the fridge if you're thirsty."

King's reply floated up the stairs. "I'm way ahead of you, MacGruder."

She smiled when she heard the crack of a soda can being opened. There was something reassuring about a man who felt at home in her kitchen.

"That reminds me." She moved to the doorway as she struggled to slide the post of an earring into the tiny hole in her earlobe. "You have that follow-up conversation with David yet?"

"This afternoon," came the response.

"And?"

"He's still wanting to quit baseball."

Peyton blew out a breath and smiled when the stubborn earring slipped into position. The second one cooperated easily, and after a quick glance in the mirror, she realized she was ready for what King had promised would be a special evening. Basic black dress, pearl necklace, discreet pearl earrings . . . the look she'd been going for was *elegant*.

She stepped out of her bedroom and began to walk down the stairs. "You want me to talk to David? I don't know much about boys or baseball, but I've heard kids will sometimes open up to an adult who isn't their parent."

"That'd be—" King moved out of the kitchen and stopped at the bottom of the staircase. His appreciative gaze raked over her and the smile on his face broadened—"fantastic."

She stopped at the bottom of the steps and breathed in the scent of his cologne. "What's fantastic—that I speak to David or my dress?"

His gaze traveled over her face and probed her eyes. "Both. With emphasis on the dress. You become more beautiful every time I see you."

Maybe she *had* achieved a smidgen of elegance. She dipped her knee in a small curtsy. "Why, thank you, kind sir. You look rather handsome yourself." She tilted her head, approving of his suit, the silk tie, and the silver cuff links at his sleeves. "Call me old-fashioned, but I believe no outfit flatters a man like a well-fitting suit. Now tell me—why is this such a special occasion?"

"That all depends on you." His voice softened, and his eyes, when she looked up, had filled with question.

"On me?" Smiling, she searched his face. "Am I missing something?"

"I sincerely hope so." He reached into his coat pocket and withdrew a small box. A jeweler's box. Not the flat, wide box that usually held a necklace or the long, rectangular box commonly used for bracelets and watches. This box was almost square, neat and tidy, and she knew what it contained before he lifted the lid.

Her mouth went dry as she stared at the sparkling diamond solitaire. "Oh, King."

"What do you think?"

Was that hope or confidence in his voice?

"It's gorgeous." She lifted her hand but couldn't bring herself to touch the ring. "It's simply beautiful."

"Just like the woman I hope will accept it. I was going to do this later, maybe after dinner, but the sight of you—well, you took my breath away, MacGruder, and I didn't want to wait a minute longer."

"King—"

He placed his fingers on her lips, stopping the words. "Let me do this, will you? I'd get down on one knee, but too many sports injuries preclude that possibility. So I'm just going to come out with it." A flush brightened his face, as if the prospect of what he was about to do had caused younger blood to fill his veins. "MacGruder—Peyton—will you marry me?"

His gaze bored into her in silent expectation, sending phantom spiders up and over the ladder of her spine. Marriage? Why would he want to marry her? He was an award-winning journalist, a top editor at the paper, and one of the most eligible bachelors in town. She had nothing to offer him but a bundle of insecurities and a haphazard past. They'd had good times together and they could have more, but *marriage*? She was no good at marriage. And she had no experience at all with being a stepmother.

She swallowed hard and tore her gaze from the diamond. After a moment of hesitation, her eyes met his. "You know I love you, right? You do know that?"

A half smile crossed his face. "I know that . . . and if your next sentence is going to start with the word *but*, I want to cash in any brownie points I may have earned over the past few weeks."

Her smile wavered. "Save those brownie points, okay? You deserve 'em."

"But?"

She inhaled a deep breath. How could she do this? If she refused him outright, he might be so hurt he'd want to sever their relationship completely. Yet though she loved him enough to not want to marry him, she was selfish enough to not want to lose him.

Which left her with only one option. "King . . . I need some time to think about it, okay?"

"What's to think about?"

How could she explain without inviting pity or false reassurances? If she unburdened her heart, he'd only protest and say all the things lovers always say when they're still wearing rose-colored glasses. She'd heard those illusory assurances before.

Her thoughts turned toward Christine. Being a parent, King ought to understand her obligation to her daughter. And she had promised that nothing would interfere with that relationship.

She gave him a brief, distracted glance and tried to smile. "I have to think about Christine."

"I don't see what—"

"She's fragile," Peyton interrupted. "She's trying to be strong, but she's still grieving and adjusting to a new reality. The kid's lost both of the people who raised her. She'll never know her biological father. I'm the only family she has left, and we barely know each other."

King's jaw flexed. "I don't mean to be insensitive, but how would our getting married affect Christine? You'll always be her mother."

She closed her eyes, unable to stand the sight of confusion and hurt on his face. "I don't know. That's one of the things I need to figure out. That's why I need time."

She heard the jeweler's box close with a muted snap, followed by King's heavy sigh. She opened her eyes and pressed her hands to his dear face. "Thank you, Kingston Danville, for considering me worthy of the honor of being your wife. And for having the patience to wait while I try to find an answer."

Or a way to help you understand that you don't want to marry me.

She kissed him, and after they pulled apart, she rested her cheek against his shoulder, grateful for the warmth of his embrace. But these demonstrations of her affection did nothing to lift the heaviness in his expression or the dejected slant of his shoulders.

Despite her best intentions, she had hurt him deeply. But accepting his proposal would have meant inflicting a far deeper wound.

Four

AFTER A RESTLESS night in which she saw King's pained face every time she closed her eyes, Peyton ate breakfast, left the house, and drove downtown to the Vintage Groove. She parked a block away and hurried toward the store, mindful of her 11:30 a.m. deadline. She probably shouldn't be making this visit at all, but she had an irresistible urge to talk to Christine . . . and this time, a phone call wouldn't do.

She looked through the wide glass windows and saw Christine standing on the customers' side of the counter. Opposite her, the generously tattooed Mike Somebody-or-other was bent over playing cards spread out near the cash register.

Must be a slow morning at the record store.

Peyton paused on the sidewalk, half-hiding behind a faded concert poster, and studied the young man behind the bar. *Man* was certainly the operative word, as nothing boyish remained in the guy's features. He had to be at least twenty-five or twenty-six, much too old for Christine.

But she hadn't come here to talk about Christine's love life.

Sighing, she pasted on a smile and opened the door.

As the bells above the door jingled, Christine looked up and grinned. "Hey! This is perfect timing, 'cause I was just about to call you."

"Really?" Peyton moved toward the register. "What's up?"

Christine leaned on the counter, eagerness bubbling in her eyes. "Remember how I said that I've been thinking about my future?"

Peyton nodded, hoping that these plans had nothing to do with Mr. Tattoo.

Christine picked up a slim paperback book and waved it before Peyton's eyes. "Ta-da! A course catalog from NC State. I checked with the admissions office, and they said that since I enrolled before the plane crash, I don't need to reapply. Cool, huh?"

Peyton offered a half smile and tried to put the pieces together. "So . . . now that you've given life a little time to settle down, you're ready to go back to school?"

"Right. I was thinking about registering for a couple of summer courses."

"That's very cool." Peyton's shoulders relaxed in relief. She looked pointedly at Mike, waiting for him to either join the conversation or excuse himself, but the man just stood there, staring at her through a fringe of greasy hair.

Christine must have read her mind. "Um, you remember Mike, right?"

Peyton nodded. "Of course."

"Mike, have you officially met my mother?"

Finally Mr. Tattoo spoke up. "Hey."

Peyton lifted a brow, waiting, but Mike didn't say or do anything else. After a moment of awkward silence, she turned to Christine. "Listen, there's something I need to talk to you about." She let her words hang for a moment; then she leaned on the counter and smiled at Mike. "Would you mind excusing us for a few minutes?"

"Not a problem." He lifted both hands in a don't-shoot pose as he took the hint. "I got some stuff to sort through in the back. Shout out if a customer comes in, and I'll deal with 'em."

"Thanks," Peyton murmured.

As Mike walked away, Christine hopped up and sat on the counter, her face a study in seriousness. "Now you've got me curious—what's so important that you had to come over here to talk to me?"

Peyton swallowed as a wave of uncertainty washed over her. Suddenly her news felt inconsequential and trivial, the sort of thing an adolescent girl might whisper to a friend in between classes. Heat flooded her face as she lowered her gaze. "King proposed to me last night."

She waited, watching through lowered lashes as the words took hold in Christine's consciousness. The girl's eyes widened, her lips parted, and the hint of color left her cheeks. Then a wall rose up behind her eyes, a defensive shield that blocked all the emotions Peyton wanted to understand.

"Did you say yes?" Christine's voice had gone flat.

"I said I'd have to think about it."

Her mouth took on an unpleasant twist. "Well, that makes

sense, since you guys have only been dating seriously for what—a couple of months?"

"Three months. But we've worked together for years."

"Still, three months isn't exactly an eternity. I've left clothes at the dry cleaner longer than that."

Peyton's smile trembled. Christine's lack of enthusiasm could not be more pronounced.

"His proposal surprised me, too." Peyton lowered her voice. "I didn't know King was ready to make that kind of a commitment. After all, he has David to think of. I do adore him, but—"

"What's not to adore? King's great, and for an older guy, he's kinda cute. I just . . ."

"What?"

Her daughter shifted her gaze to the windows at the front of the store. "I don't know. Nothing."

Peyton leaned closer. "Come on, spit it out. What are you thinking right now?"

Christine shrugged, but Peyton stood close enough to feel a subterranean shiver pass through her. "I'm just a little afraid . . . of getting squeezed out of the family album, I guess."

"Chris." Peyton took her daughter's hand. "I didn't accept. But even if I had, you should know that nothing will ever change my love for you."

Christine managed a wavering smile. "Right. Of course not. I'm just being selfish."

"You're being normal." Peyton drew the girl's slender frame into her arms. "But you needn't worry. I promised to be around for you, and I intend to keep that promise."

"Thanks." Christine's breath warmed Peyton's ear. "But whatever you decide is cool. It's your life, so do what you want to do."

Peyton pulled away and studied her daughter's worried eyes. Brave words, coming from a girl who'd been recently orphaned. She'd become accustomed to loss, so hardened to it . . . she probably thought that losing Peyton was inevitable.

Maybe it was, in the long view. People aged, time passed, and death often arrived when least expected. But Peyton had already abandoned this girl once. She would not do it again.

"I will never do what's right for me without thinking about what's right for *you*." Peyton brushed a sheaf of hair out of Christine's eye. "We are a team, baby girl. You and me. And don't you ever forget it."

Yet as they exchanged a smile and another hug, Peyton couldn't help remembering the pain in King's eyes and the wariness in his parting embrace. She hadn't meant to hurt him, hadn't wanted to change the status of their relationship. She could have continued as they were for months, enjoying his company, working with him at the office, loving him at arm's length . . .

Why did love have to demand more than she could possibly give?

Peyton's talk with Christine took longer than she'd planned, so by the time she arrived at the office, she was only an hour away from deadline. For once Mandi wasn't keeping vigil by the elevator, and Peyton was able to slip into her cubicle largely unnoticed. She dropped her purse into her desk drawer, then stood behind her chair, sorting through her priorities.

Before she could sit down, Nora's head and shoulders loomed over the cubicle wall. "You owe me a column and a special features article."

Peyton winced. "Yeah, I know. I'm on it."

"How's the anniversary feature coming along?"

"Are you sure you want that 'life lessons' piece? I was thinking about adapting my idea for an article on parenting older adolescents—"

"Not going to fly. Unless you're planning to interview several experts, you're not qualified to write a piece like that. You're falling into your old habits, Peyton. People don't want facts and quotes from you, they want to hear from your *heart*."

Peyton snapped her mouth shut, stunned by the editor's bluntness.

"Listen," Nora softened her voice, "the parenting article is a good idea, but you're not the one to write it. If you were a family expert or if you had years of parenting experience, I'd have a different opinion. But you don't, so why not do the life lessons piece?"

Peyton shrugged and sank into her chair. "Okay, if that's what you want. No problem."

"Good." Nora leaned forward, her face alive with curiosity. "So . . . what *are* some of the lessons you've learned?"

Peyton resisted the urge to grimace. "Um . . ." She scanned her brain and reached for the first thought that popped to the surface. "I've learned that people are divided on the caution versus passion issue. Some naturally follow their passions; others look to caution and reason before making a decision."

"And you're in the caution camp?"

"Definitely."

The editor shook her head. "I think your readers already know that about you. Find another topic, a less predictable angle."

Peyton blew out a breath and glanced around her desk, then spied Eve Miller's name on a memo pad. "Okay—how about a piece where I take the opposite tack, trumpeting passion over caution?"

Nora lifted a brow. "Are you planning on playing devil's advocate?"

"Not necessarily. I'll say I'm switching sides to evaluate things from another perspective. Trying to determine the right time to take a chance on love."

"What's the hook?"

"Opposing opinion from a reader."

Nora considered a moment; then her mouth twisted in something not quite a smile. "Flesh it out and get back to me with a proposal. This is your moment to shine, so don't blow it."

Peyton exhaled as the editor walked away. Who had time to think about life lessons when all the hours of a day were claimed by items on life *lists*? She had several pressing tasks on her list now—she had to write a column in an hour. And talk to David for King. And help Christine clean out her father's closet. And decide how to turn down King's marriage proposal without destroying their relationship. Oh yes, and write a dazzling feature article strong enough to land a syndication contract.

Not small assignments, any of them, but only one was due within the hour.

She sank into her chair and pulled out a copy of the ideas she'd compiled for this month's columns. Among the summaries she'd sent to Nora was a piece on St. Patrick, but St. Paddy's Day was still over a week away. That left the topics of springtime, the origin of the saying "March comes in like a lion and goes out like a lamb," a tongue-in-cheek piece on how to establish your own country, and several other topics that didn't particularly excite her.

She turned to her computer and opened her e-mail program, scanning the list of reader letters to see if any of them had posed a question worth answering in print. No—apart from Eve Miller, no one else had sent in an idea worth following up.

The Heart Healer was scraping the bottom of the barrel.

She went back to her ideas memo and plucked one—micronations—from the list. Anyone who had ever shared her sudden longing to run away should find the idea interesting.

She swiveled toward her computer again and opened her word processing program.

Had it up to here with city hall? Tired of battling your neighborhood's homeowners' association? Feeling swamped by your personal to-do list?

Declare yourself free of imposed regulations and expectations by declaring yourself a citizen—even the ruler—of your own country. All you need is unclaimed territory—real or imagined—a government, a constitution, a few citizens, and a flag. The country you create will join other free and independent micronations. As long as you dwell in your micronation, you will be free to live—

"So—you finally made it in!"

Startled, Peyton looked up and saw her intern standing in front of her desk.

"Mandi!" She assumed her most plaintive expression. "Nora's breathing down my neck, and she's going to want details on that anniversary feature from me soon. Please tell me you got ahold of Eve Miller."

The girl blinked. "If I told you that, I'd be lying."

"You still have the envelope, right? and her letter?"

"It's at my desk."

"Then get me the address, please. If you don't reach her by the end of the day, maybe I'll drop by her house. If I don't catch her, I can always leave a note in the door."

Mandi hurried away to fetch the letter while Peyton reached for a pen. One more item for the to-do list, but at least visiting Eve Miller was a tangible task. After she'd interviewed the woman, she'd be able to write the feature article and cross another item off her list. If only she could handle the situations with King and David and Christine as easily . . .

But people couldn't be crossed off a list. Relationships couldn't be shelved, they couldn't be delegated, and they couldn't even be postponed for very long.

And she had never been very good at relationships.

After filing her column and taking a well-earned coffee break, Peyton walked by King's office. The door stood ajar, an open invitation, but she could see him hunched over his keyboard, his fingers pounding the keys and his gaze glued to the screen. She exhibited the same kind of concentration when the writing was going well. When it wasn't . . . well, on those occasions, she never minded an interruption.

Maybe King wouldn't mind one now. Even if he did, she really needed to talk to him about what happened last night. He had to understand that her unwillingness to accept his proposal had nothing to do with him and everything to do with her.

She rapped on the doorframe and smiled when he lifted his head. "Sorry to interrupt," she called, leaning into the office. "Do you have a minute?"

"For you? Always." She saw no trace of hurt in his welcoming grin. He turned from the computer and gestured to the empty chair before his desk. "What's up?"

She closed the door behind her and took the proffered chair. "I wanted to tell you how much I enjoyed the play last night."

He chuckled. "Me, too. Especially the last act."

"But you slept through the last act."

"My point exactly."

Peyton hesitated, holding her coffee mug between both hands as she searched for words.

"Uh-oh." King's easygoing smile flattened out. "That's not a good sign."

"What?"

"That line between your brows. But never mind. Tell me . . . any news on the decision front?"

She frowned, annoyed by his bright confidence. He was behaving as if he expected her to accept his proposal as soon as she'd had a good night's sleep. "King, you proposed less than twenty-four hours ago."

"That's not enough time to figure out if you love someone?"

"It's not enough time—" she paused, choosing her words with care—"to figure out if you can properly balance your life. If you can be fair to everyone involved."

Annoyance struggled with humor on his tanned face as he studied her. "MacGruder, only two people are involved here—you and me."

"That's not true. And while I'm not exactly a social butterfly, I do have other people to consider before making such an important decision."

"MacGruder, you live with two cats."

"I have a daughter, and you have a son. And I don't know the first thing about being a stepmother."

"You don't have to be David's mother. The boy is twenty; he's already been brought up. All you have to do is be my wife."

"David's not the only child involved." She set her coffee mug on the edge of his desk. "I drove downtown to talk to Christine this morning."

His left brow rose a fraction. "And?"

Peyton shrugged. "She did her best to act happy about it. She even said you were cute, for an old guy. But I think the idea of sharing me has her pretty freaked out."

King brought his hand to his chin. "Are you sure you're not overrating her reaction? Kids are resilient, you know—they adjust."

"Christine has done nothing *but* adjust lately, and I don't want to traumatize her further. She and I are just beginning to build our relationship. It terrifies me to think I might damage it."

King's mouth spread into a thin-lipped smile. "You think marriage to me would do damage?"

"Look," Peyton added, "I think we both need to give our kids our full attention. Solidify those relationships. Afterward, when things with David and Christine have settled down, we can refocus on ourselves and see where things are heading."

"Peyton—"

Her cell phone beeped, cutting him off. She pulled the phone from her pocket and glanced at the caller ID screen. "That's David, returning my text. He's good to meet me for lunch. I promised to pick up sandwiches."

King leaned back in his chair, his face set in lines of weary resignation. "Have a great time. I hope you get things settled with my son, at least."

"I'll try my best." Peyton stood, reluctant to go, but needing to be on her way to meet David.

"Oh, by the way." King gestured toward the phone. "My buddy in New York called this morning. Turns out the *Times* is looking for a new sports editor. Apparently I made the short list."

Peyton halted as unease nipped at the back of her neck. "Is . . . is that something you'd consider?"

"It's a logical next step in my career. After all, it's the *New York Times*."

"But—you'd move to *Manhattan*?"

He shrugged. "Look, the short list isn't an offer. I'm not going to worry about it until I have to, okay? You shouldn't, either."

She nodded, astounded by the fact that King would even consider taking a job in New York. But if she turned down his proposal, how could she blame him for wanting to start a new chapter in his life?

"Go on." King waved her out the door. "Go solidify my relationship with my son, will you? So you and I can move on to refocusing on *us*."

Peyton twiddled her fingers in a wave, but outside King's office she stopped by the watercooler and leaned against the wall, more confused than ever. She had gone to King's office to help him see that she couldn't possibly marry him, but she'd come out charged with talking to his son so they could marry sooner rather than later. How had things become so turned around?

Because King was so overwhelmingly confident, that's how. Because he believed in her, in their relationship, so much that he couldn't see the pitfalls on the road ahead. One of the things she loved best about him was his unflappable optimism, but at some point, one of them needed to take the realistic view.

She found it all too easy to get caught up in King's enthusiasm, to listen to her heart instead of her head. One thing was certain: over the next few days, either her head or her heart would have to retreat and remain silent. She would keep her promise to King and David; she'd keep her word to Christine. She'd get her anniversary feature done and try her best to make Nora happy. The syndication issue was out of her hands; either the syndicate people would like her or they wouldn't.

After doing her best at trying to keep so many people happy, she'd stand back and wait to see what King decided about New York. Because the *Times* would definitely want him; any newspaper would. He was an incredible writer, a skilled editor, and a compassionate manager.

And quite possibly the love of her life.

When he had gone, Peyton would dry her tears, blow her nose, and get back to work.

Just as she always had.

Five

BY THE TIME Peyton arrived at the university, her sense of nervousness had gelled into a solid lump in her stomach. What did she know about counseling adolescents? For that matter, what did she know about David? She'd met him only a couple of times, and their conversations had been brief and general. She'd volunteered to talk to him because she wanted to help King, but some part of her had hoped he'd brush off her offer.

She didn't even know much about baseball.

She met David, King's son from his first marriage, outside the college library, where he gallantly offered to help her carry the blanket and sandwiches she'd picked up on her drive to the school. She accepted his help and walked beside him, aware that he received more than a few admiring glances from passing girls as they strolled to one of the commons. David looked very much like his father—the same strong jaw, curly brown hair, tall frame. But King's face had been etched with the dignified lines of passing years, some of them hard, while David's was still as smooth as sculpted marble. One day he would be as handsome as his father . . . but not yet.

David pointed to a sunny spot of grass at a distance from the sidewalk. "How about here?"

"Perfect. It's too pretty a day to eat inside." Peyton took the blanket and spread it out, noticing that other students were doing the same thing. The winter had been long and bitter, but spring promised to be glorious. Though a chill remained in the air, the sky overhead was a perfect curve of blue and the lawn shimmered with sunlight.

The warm sunshine helped thaw the lump in Peyton's gut as she sat on the blanket and pulled deli sandwiches from a paper bag. So far, so good; David seemed to be at ease around her, and that helped calm her anxiety. He sat beside her, his blue-jeaned legs stretched over the blanket and his face tipped toward the sky.

"I appreciate your taking the time to meet me," she said, setting a pastrami sandwich by David's side. "I know how busy college students can be."

He shrugged—the gesture a carbon copy of King's—and accepted the sandwich. "First lesson I learned in school: never pass up a free meal."

"Not entirely free, I'm afraid. You're going to have to put up with the third degree about why you quit baseball."

A rueful smile flickered across his face. "I figured that's what this was about. Dad's enlisted you in the cause."

"Not really." Peyton pulled out her own sandwich and began to unwrap it. "I don't care whether you play ball or not. But I do care about you and your dad. I'm worried about you guys."

"What's to worry about?"

"You two don't seem to be able to communicate. He says you don't talk. You say he doesn't listen."

He pulled the cellophane from his meal. "Yeah, well, it's always been like that with us."

"Always?"

"Since he and my mom got divorced, anyway." David took a bite of his sandwich and chewed slowly.

Peyton drew a deep breath. She ought to be able to handle this—she was, after all, the Heart Healer. But typing out a reply gleaned from perusing professional counseling books was much easier than looking into the wounded eyes of a young man and attempting to give advice.

"Well," she ventured, "maybe it's time you go back to what your relationship used to be. I mean, you can't ignore what happened, but don't get hung up on it. Find some middle ground and build a new relationship from there."

He squinted at her but kept chewing.

Her reply had probably sounded far too glib. What was the heart of the problem?

"You know," she added, almost as an afterthought, "your father would do anything for you."

David snorted. "Except pay my tuition."

"Did he say that?"

"Not exactly. No. But it doesn't really matter. Not anymore."

Peyton stared, unable to make sense of his statement. "You'd better explain that one."

"I didn't just quit baseball. I quit school."

"*What?*"

"I'm not into it anymore," he went on, the words coming out double-time. "Haven't been all year. That's why my grades stink. That's why I stopped going to classes. And that's why they cut me from the team."

"They *cut* you?"

David gave her a humorless smile. "Dad's gonna have a stroke when he finds out, but I don't care. This—" he gestured to the stately buildings around them—"just isn't my thing. Not anymore."

Peyton drew a deep breath and struggled to maintain control of her emotions. She'd be furious if she'd scrimped and saved to send Christine to college and then found out that the girl had dropped out without warning. Without giving Peyton a chance to help or find out what went wrong.

"So you're not into school anymore," she said, her voice sounding strangled in her own ears. "What *is* your thing these days?"

David studied his sandwich for a moment, then looked sideways at Peyton. "You may not believe me."

"Give me a chance."

"Okay. I'm into art now."

"Excuse me?"

"I want to go to art school in California. CalArts."

Her mouth went dry. "So far away?"

His eyes narrowed. "It's not like I was living at home."

He was right, of course. Even before college, he hadn't been living with King. The divorce had not only ended a marriage, it had nearly severed the relationship between King and his only son. For months they didn't talk, and later they only talked about "safe" topics. Like the weather. And sports.

"Okay, let's back up." Peyton's eyes caught and held David's. "You want to be an artist."

He straightened his shoulders. "Sort of. Yeah. I mean, what's wrong with that?"

"Nothing, I just didn't know you had any interest in art. I don't think your dad does, either."

"Yeah? Well, I do."

Peyton gripped his shoulder and lowered her head to look into his eyes. "If that's your passion, you should pursue it, okay? I'm on your side in this."

He snorted. "Think you can convince my dad?"

She chuckled. "Oh no. That's your job. You're his son, so you have to talk to him yourself." She smiled, waiting for his response, but David's eyes remained remote and inscrutable.

"I'm not going to say anything to King about this because this is a matter between the two of you. But the sooner you deal with this, David, the better off—the happier—you'll be."

"I've already tried to talk to him. Every time I bring it up, he goes ballistic."

"Maybe you need to let him vent. Don't walk out on him; give him time to express his feelings, too. Then try again."

He looked away for a long moment, then gave her an uncertain nod. "Okay. I'll talk to him again. But I don't know how he's going to take it."

"Have a little faith in him, okay? After all, you're asking him to have faith in you."

He crossed his legs and stared moodily into the distance. "I guess you're right."

"I'm glad you think so." She pulled another container from the plastic bag. "You like potato salad? I hope so, because I bought two pints of the stuff."

ॐ

The sun had begun to dip toward the western horizon by the time Peyton located the stately brick home that matched Eve Miller's address. The house lay in a quiet part of town occupied by older residents and even older buildings. Shrubs outlined each front lawn, hedges that would be lush and green in summer but now stood bare and skeletal in the gathering gloom.

Yellow rectangles of lamplight brightened the facades of several houses, but no lights shone in the Miller home. The driveway stood empty, as did the graveled parking spot outside the wrought iron fence, but Eve Miller's vehicle might be tucked into the narrow garage. . . .

Peyton parked across the street and felt a memory brush past her, as gentle as the touch of moth wings. Her father had lived in a neighborhood like this. She had lived with him until her mother died, but then, due to the demands of his medical practice, he had sent Peyton to boarding school. The on-campus nurse resided in a house like this one, with black shutters at the windows, a small front porch, and tenacious ivy blanketing the south side. Peyton had spent many hours in that small house, battling homesickness and other illnesses both real and imagined. . . .

Why was she thinking of that now?

She shook off the memory, double-checked the house number, and slid out of her car. Before she could cross to the garden gate, a woman on a bicycle rounded the corner. The trim woman wore sneakers, a long skirt, gloves, and a maroon peacoat. Peyton waited, allowing the bicyclist time to pass, but the woman stopped at Eve Miller's house and propped the bike against the fence.

Peyton fingered the wool collar at her throat and studied the rider more closely. The woman beneath the knitted cap might be anywhere from thirty to seventy, impossible to tell from this distance. Tendrils of blonde hair floated around her unlined face, while a fuzzy scarf enveloped her neck. She fussed for a moment with a basket fastened to the back of the bike; then she slipped the basket over her arm and strode toward the front door with long, determined strides.

"Mrs. Miller?" Peyton caught her breath when the woman halted and turned. "Sorry to interrupt, but I'm Peyton MacGruder—"

"I see you got my note," the woman answered, dipping her chin in an abrupt nod. She turned again and strode to the front door, keys jangling as she unlocked the house and stepped over the threshold.

Peyton stood in the road, blinking, and finally found the courage to advance. She was halfway up the garden path when she heard the woman's voice again: "If you want to punch me in the nose, Ms. MacGruder, you're going to have to come inside to do it."

Peyton grinned. This interview promised to be interesting.

She stepped through the open door and stared in surprise. Instead of the dark foyer she'd been expecting, Eve Miller's front door led to an airy studio filled with light and deep, vibrant colors. Royal blue walls provided a striking backdrop for several ceramic pieces displayed on wooden shelving. A potter's wheel occupied the center of the space, and a dark kiln stood at the back of the room. Several paintings had been grouped around a large east-facing window, one of them appearing to be a portrait of the lady herself.

Eve stood before a small desk, peering at a blinking telephone as she shrugged out of a coat that seemed to be made of a rich tapestry.

"I'm sorry to show up unannounced," Peyton said. "I tried to call several times."

The beginning of a smile tipped the corners of Eve's mouth. "Been at my daughter's in Raleigh."

Peyton gestured to the front of the house. "You, um, rode your bike to Raleigh?"

"Of course not. I took the bus. I rode my bike to the station." She gestured to a kettle on a hot plate. "Tea?"

Peyton shrugged. "If you're having some."

As Eve Miller took the kettle into another room, presumably the kitchen, Peyton moved to the desk, where several photographs stood in antique frames. One photo featured an attractive young woman and two big-eyed children. The children resembled the woman, sharing her brown eyes and dimples in their chins.

Peyton held up the picture. "Is this your daughter?"

Eve came back into the room, kettle in hand. "Yes, that's Dawn. And those two precious darlings with her are my grandchildren."

Peyton set the photo back in place and picked up another frame. This one featured a picture of a much younger Eve and three men in uniform. One was African American, one was strong-jawed and brown-haired, and the other, a sandy-haired man with a wide smile, had his arm draped around Eve's shoulders. The foursome stood next to a sign that read, "Newport News Naval Air Station."

Peyton tapped the photo. "This your husband?"

Eve didn't bother to look. "Billy's the one with his arm around me."

"He was a pilot?"

"Copilot." Eve moved to stand beside Peyton and pointed first to the African American soldier, then to the third man. "Richie Franks was the loadmaster; Ben Morrick was the pilot. They flew rescue helicopters. They were all part of the same crew and still training in '66 when that picture was taken."

Peyton looked for other pictures of the sandy-haired man but found none. "You and Billy still married?"

"Billy died when my daughter was four. Years ago—so many I've lost count."

"I'm sorry to hear that. Was he killed in the war?"

"Ben and Richie went to Vietnam, but Billy stayed behind. He . . ." She shook her head, then smiled and pointed toward a small sofa against the wall. "Why don't you have a seat. You can tell me a bit about yourself while we wait for the water to boil."

Peyton sat on the edge of the sofa and placed her hands in her lap. She had never felt comfortable exposing her personal life to strangers; one of the reasons she had become a reporter was so she could ask questions and not have to answer them. But a good interviewer had to be able to make small talk well enough to put subjects at ease.

"My husband passed away, too," she said, glancing down at her hands. "As you said, it was years ago—so many I've lost count. We have something else in common—I also have a daughter."

When she looked up and met Eve's gaze, she was struck by the look of intense curiosity in the woman's eyes.

"I suppose I should begin at the beginning," Eve said, her expression shifting to one of faint amusement. "You should know that I read your column religiously."

Peyton smiled. "That's appropriate, because I'm always praying that I won't write something stupid."

"Then you must have slipped up on your prayers, because last week you said something truly idiotic. That's when I sent you a note. I had begun to think you'd only had a momentary lapse, but then you did it again. In yesterday's column you repeated your mistake, insisting—how did you put it? That a happy heart is a cautious heart."

"I was quoting one of the ancient Greeks." Peyton lifted her chin. "And I happen to agree with—"

Eve cut her off with a soft laugh. "Then Eumenides was a fool, too. Let me offer a counter quote: 'Only passions, great passions, can elevate the soul to great things.' Surely you've heard *that* before."

Peyton closed her eyes. "Can't say that I have."

"Diderot," Eve said, her voice low and self-assured.

"But that isn't a relevant rebuttal. Passion in a career, in art, in music, is certainly to be commended. But love always involves another person, so it certainly pays to approach with caution."

"Doesn't perfect love cast out fear?"

"Fear and caution are not the same thing."

"Aren't they . . . in certain situations, at least?" Eve quirked her brow and folded her arms. "And now I have to wonder—with so much in common, why do we find ourselves at odds on the question of when to trust our hearts instead of listening to our heads?"

Peyton felt a smile twist the corner of her mouth. "That's exactly what I'm hoping to learn by interviewing you."

"Interviewing me?"

"For a special feature celebrating my first year as the Heart Healer. My editor and I thought it might be fun to explore an opposing viewpoint."

A shrill whistle from the teakettle interrupted the conversation. Eve stood and removed it from the heating element. "I'm not interested in being interviewed, Ms. MacGruder."

Peyton blinked. "But your note—your invitation—"

"Was for a discussion. An exchange over a cup of tea."

"An exchange?"

"Of stories and life lessons." She gave a mischievous smile. "Perhaps even a secret or two."

A flicker of apprehension coursed through Peyton as she shook her head. "A discussion isn't going to help me meet my deadline. I need an interview and I think my readers will be interested in you."

"But I'm interested in *you*. I read your columns and find myself wondering what could have led you to arrive at the conclusions you have reached. Give and take, Ms. MacGruder. I want an equal exchange of ideas and personal histories. That way we'll both gain something."

Peyton swallowed hard, feeling suddenly vulnerable beneath the woman's intense gaze. "I'm afraid I misunderstood. I'm sorry to have wasted your time." She stood and stepped toward the door.

"I'll be here," Eve called, filling a mug with steaming water. "If you change your mind."

Six

THE NEXT MORNING, Peyton found Mandi waiting by her cubicle. "Well?" the intern asked, practically dancing in excitement. "How'd it go with Eve Miller?"

Peyton sighed and dropped her briefcase onto her desk. "Not so well."

"Is she a nutcase?"

"She's an eccentric, maybe, and an artist, but she's not nuts. In any case, she wouldn't agree to an interview."

"Then why'd she—"

"Tea. She wrote because she wanted to have tea with me."

"That's nuts."

"Actually, she was quite sane and quite classy. But I don't have time to accept social invitations. Now, if you'll excuse me, there's a certain sports editor I need to see." Peyton stepped around the intern and headed toward King's office.

"Um . . . ," Mandi called. "He's not in there."

Peyton halted in midstride and turned. "Where'd he go?"

"Don't know. But steam was shooting from his ears when he blew outta here about ten minutes ago."

Peyton sighed heavily, pivoted on the ball of her foot, and returned to her desk. She picked up her phone and punched the speed dial. "Hey, you've reached King's cell phone," a warm voice buzzed in her ear. "You know what to do at the beep."

She turned, folding one arm across her chest. "King, it's me. I wanted to talk to you before you spoke to David, but I have a feeling I'm too late. I thought you'd call last night, so when you didn't . . . Anyway, call or stop by my desk later so I can fill you in."

She dropped the phone back into its cradle and glanced at Mandi, who was examining clippings on her bulletin board and pretending not to listen. "Mandi, I have a project for you. Would you please go down to the morgue and see what you can dig up on Eve Miller or her husband?"

"But you said—"

"His name was Billy Miller, probably William. He died . . . must have been the early seventies."

Mandi pulled out her steno pad and made a note. "You're the boss."

Peyton watched as Mandi trotted away; then she sank into her chair and closed her eyes. Why did she feel exhausted at ten in the morning? Maybe it had something to do with King and David and Christine and the column that Had Not Materialized but was due by noon.

Last night she'd spent so much time puzzling over her talk with Eve Miller that she hadn't given much thought to her upcoming column, but this one would be published in the Sunday paper, which drew twice as many readers as the weekday edition. So she needed to sift through her ideas and find something particularly strong—

"Mom?"

Peyton blinked at the unfamiliar word and looked up at her daughter, who stood in the aisle outside her cubicle. "Christine?"

"You okay? You look worried."

Peyton forced a smile. "Busted. But I'm okay; I was just thinking about my column—and my deadline." She halted as worry seized her by the throat—Christine hardly ever came to the newspaper office. What could be wrong?

Her eyes searched Christine's face for signs of distress. "What's up?"

Christine stepped closer. "I wanted to talk to you about something. Got a minute?"

Peyton's heart reacted again as anxiety clamored for her attention. "For you, always. Do you . . ." She glanced around the open cubicle, wondering if she should take her daughter someplace more private.

"It'll only take a minute." Christine's eyes warmed as she smiled. "I've been thinking a lot about you and me and King and the whole marriage thing. I have to tell you, I was pretty stressed about it."

Peyton gazed into her daughter's face. "Trust me, that makes two of us."

"So . . . have you decided anything yet?"

Peyton shook her head. "I'm still sorting things out."

"Okay, then, what I wanted to tell you is that you shouldn't let me be the thing that keeps you and King apart. I mean, don't let me, our relationship, be the reason you decide not to hook up with King, okay? Just leave me out of the equation."

"I can't do that." Peyton spread her hands. "You are part of my life, so I can't leave you out. I don't want to do anything that would hurt you—"

"Your being married wouldn't hurt me. I can deal with you being married, but I can't deal with you resenting me, even a little. Okay?"

Peyton took a deep breath as a dozen different emotions collided. She'd been right to worry, but apparently Christine considered herself mature enough to handle it. Was she? Or was this brave speech just an act?

She gave her daughter a reluctant smile. "Thanks. That assurance means a lot to me."

Christine grabbed the strap of her shoulder bag and moved toward the aisle. "Look, I gotta go. Gotta get to work."

"Chris," Peyton called, stopping her. "I love you."

"I love you, too." Christine smiled and headed out, but the spring was still missing from her step. Sure, she'd said she'd be okay with the marriage—just like Peyton always said she was *okay* when another reporter got the promotion or the award she'd been working for. Sometimes you painted on a happy face and forced yourself to say all the right things. Sometimes once the words were out of your mouth you could even believe them.

But people often fed themselves lies when accepting the truth would hurt too much, and Christine knew it would hurt Peyton to turn down King's proposal. So she'd convinced herself that she'd be fine with the marriage, even while her heart had to be twisting at the thought of sharing her newfound mother with a man who would be closer than she could ever be.

Peyton watched her daughter step into the elevator before she picked up the phone again and dialed King's number. After a moment, the familiar voice filled her ear: "Hey, you've reached King's cell phone . . ."

She lowered the phone when Mandi approached, a folder in her hand. "Eve Miller was married to William Stanhope Miller. Known to friends as Billy. Wealthy family from Charlotte. Made their money in the banking business."

Peyton jerked her chin toward the folder. "Did you find anything on Eve?"

"Yeah." Mandi fumbled with the file and pulled out a couple of printed copies. "Eve Jackson Miller was another country club type; her father was a judge. Mom was a debutante from Chapel Hill. Both are long dead."

"That's good background material. Anything else?"

"Oh yeah, there's tons of info. Apparently Eve Miller is a well-known artist; she's been written up in several local publications."

"Let me guess—she's a ceramicist."

"Yeah." Mandi's eyes twinkled with a how-did-you-know smile. "She has pieces in several museums, even galleries in New York, San Francisco, and Paris. She and Billy had one child."

"A daughter. Did she ever remarry?"

"I didn't see any record of a second marriage, but I didn't really look for one. There are lots of other records I could check out—"

"Thanks, but I can look them up when—*if*—I decide to quote her in that feature. Thank you, Mandi. You did good work." Peyton swiveled to face her computer, then picked up the headset she used to block the sounds of the office. "If you see King around, tell him I'll look for him at lunch. Right now, I've got to crank out a column."

"Copy that," Mandi called, waving as she headed back to her desk.

Dear Readers:

In the many years of my lifetime—a number I'll keep to myself, thank you very much—I've come to realize that we often make what I call "crossroads" decisions without even being aware of them.

How many times have you made a decision that forever changed the course of your life? If you'd chosen to study music instead of mathematics; if you'd gone out with Brad instead of Jim that summer night. How would your life be different if you'd taken the 8:10 train instead of the 9:40? Perhaps your situation wouldn't have changed at all—but if the early train had derailed en route to its destination, your life and the lives of your loved ones would have been forever altered.

Not only do our choices affect our futures, but my choices affect you—perhaps not directly, but we are all part of a vast network of roads and choices that frequently bring us to intersection and community. Sometimes our paths merge . . . and sometimes life leads us in opposite directions. We see evidence of this every day as organizations are created and disbanded, even as families form and dissolve.

Each of us travels on an individual road, but none of us travels alone. So how should we approach decisions that will affect not only us, but also the people we love?

When you come to a crossroads decision point, whom do you call for advice? Upon what criteria do you base your choices? Are you the type who goes with your gut instinct, or do you consider, research, and weigh the evidence before deciding which way to turn? How do you conquer your fears about the possible negative consequences of an unwise choice?

Perhaps our decision-making process is determined by inborn personality; perhaps it is shaped through environment. But no matter what process you employ, wise men through the ages have advised caution at these crisis points. In 1693, William Congreve advised, "Marry in haste, repent at leisure." Solomon wrote that we should "make plans by seeking advice."

In the spirit of fair play, however, I should give equal time to Benjamin Disraeli, who believed that man is "only truly great when he acts from the passions." Another man, Vauvenargues, proclaimed that "the mind is the soul's eye, not its source of power. That lies in the heart, in other words, in the passions."

I've mentioned the passion versus caution debate several times in the last few days, and now I'd be interested in hearing from you about your "crossroads choices." At those pivotal points of your life, what convinced you to move one way instead of another? Did you take, as Robert Frost described it, the road less traveled by? Was your decision more influenced by your reasoning or by your enthusiasm? Have you had regrets? If life offered you a second chance to make that choice, would you move in a different direction?

Write to me, the Heart Healer, here at the Middleborough Times. *I look forward to hearing from you.*

King didn't come back to the office after lunch. After filing her column, Peyton tried to nose around to discover if he had scheduled an interview or a meeting, but her questions about King resulted only in a rash of sly smiles and winks from her coworkers. "If you don't know where he is," one of the sportswriters joked, "who does?"

So, after jotting down a few thoughts on the joys of springtime for her Monday column, Peyton drove home. She pulled into the driveway and was halfway up the front walk when she realized she wasn't alone—David sat on her front porch swing, his motorcycle helmet on his lap. She glanced around and spied his bike parked on the side lawn. She must have had her head in the clouds not to notice *that*.

She smiled in pleased surprise as a feeling of satisfaction swept through her. Something she said yesterday must have resonated with David. Maybe she wasn't as inept as she feared.

She lifted her hand, about to greet him, but David cut her off. "I can't believe," he yelled, bridled anger in his voice, "that you told him."

Peyton halted. "Told who what?"

"My dad. You told him I got cut from the team."

She stared at him in dazed exasperation. "I didn't say a word to your father. I didn't see him last night and I haven't spoken to him all day."

"I trusted you!" David continued as if he hadn't heard her protest, his voice rising in an indignant shout. "How could you do that?"

"Didn't you hear me?" Peyton climbed the steps to the front porch and stared at her red-faced young guest. "I said I haven't seen your father all day. So why don't you calm down and tell me what happened?"

David shook his head, then glared at her with burning, reproachful eyes. "He freaked out, that's what happened. He found me at the gym this morning, cleaning out my locker. I was thinking, good, we can finally talk, but he started yelling at me, accusing me of not having any kind of work ethic, of blowing an opportunity any other kid would kill for—"

"Come on, David, I'm sure he didn't—"

"Don't defend him, okay? Because the reality is I don't care anymore! About what either of you has to say."

She reached for him, intending to place her hand on his shoulder. "David—"

He ducked away from her reach. "Stay out of my life, will you?" He rose up out of the porch swing, all six feet two inches of him, and blazed at her for a heated moment before he ran down the steps and strode across the lawn. Peyton felt her knees turn to jelly as she watched him go. Whatever made her think she knew anything about communicating with kids?

She moved toward the door, ready to give up, but King's face rose before her eyes. For him, she'd give it another try. She'd promised.

She turned, the house keys in her hand. "David, wait a minute."

He strapped on his helmet without answering.

"David, if you'd only—"

"Forget it." He threw a leg over the saddle of his bike and brought his foot down hard on the starter.

"David!" The roar of the engine drowned out Peyton's plea. King's son rode away, his back ramrod straight as the bike slanted into traffic.

Peyton looked at the keys in her hand and blinked away a sudden rush of tears. She wasn't cut out to be a stepmother. She was barely finding her way through the maze of motherhood.

And she'd never been prepared to be a wife.

She drew a deep breath and inserted the key into the lock. Maybe King had good reasons for avoiding her today. Now that she'd hurt him and alienated his son, the man was probably trying to break things off as gently as possible.

ᆭ

The wind outside had worked itself into a symphony of moans and whistles by the time Peyton finished dinner, cleared off the kitchen counter, and spread Mandi's materials across her granite work island. She lit a candle simply because she enjoyed the vanilla scent, not because it created a soft and romantic glow. Why did she need ambience? She was alone again, with only Samson and Elijah for company.

Samson, the white Persian, wound around her ankles as she made herself a cup of hot cocoa and tried to forget that it was Friday night. Until this week, she'd reserved her Friday evenings for King. Sometimes they went to local sports events; sometimes they went out to dinner and a movie; sometimes they simply stayed in and watched TV or read by the fireplace. She'd begun to take these relaxed, pleasant evenings for granted.

But today she hadn't seen King at the office, nor had he returned her calls. So wherever he was, he obviously had plans that didn't include her.

She perched on a barstool and skimmed the copied articles, many of which were more than thirty years old. She highlighted words that might help her understand Eve's background: *the Honorable Walter Jackson, elected judge, conservative constituency.* Beneath the articles, she found a photograph captioned, "Judge Walter and Mrs. Jackson, accompanied by their twelve-year-old daughter, Eve, at a black-tie charity event."

Eve had been no less charming at twelve than she was yesterday. Though Peyton could have sworn that every girl endured an ugly duckling phase sometime around the sixth grade, the preadolescent Eve Jackson looked tall, slender, and lovely in her sleeveless white gown.

The girl had probably learned how to fold napkins in her cradle.

Beneath the photo lay William "Billy" Miller's obituary and an article titled, "Boating Accident Claims Life of Local Lawyer." A photo of Billy on his sailboat ran adjacent to the headline.

Peyton jotted random thoughts on her steno pad as an idea took shape in her mind. The article would be better if Eve had agreed to an interview, but her refusal didn't mean Peyton couldn't write a feature about passion versus reason. With additional comments from her readers, the story should fill out nicely. When all was said and done, Peyton just might prove her point: when it came to making life decisions, the wise woman trusted her brain, not her emotions. Emotions were far too fickle . . . just like some people.

She dropped her pen as a surge of exasperation threatened to engulf her. Even if King was trying to break things off, he was not the type to be rude. So maybe he hadn't called because he'd been in meetings all day. Or maybe he went off this morning without his cell phone. Or maybe his car had slid off the road on his way home from the university and he was lying unconscious at the bottom of a ditch. Or maybe he hadn't forgotten his phone and he *had* heard her messages, but he was upset with her. Maybe he wanted to teach her a lesson by ignoring their usual date night because he thought she'd ignored his proposal.

Okay, but if he wanted to play adolescent games, she would

demand an explanation of the rules. Their relationship had been lovely and she would be happy for it to continue, but if he wanted to break things off, he should do so with a measure of dignity and respect. And if he wanted to traipse off to New York, she'd wish him the best in his new life and career. She'd wish him the best of everything, including a girlfriend who didn't come with so much excess baggage—

The doorbell rang, and she stiffened. With pulse-pounding certainty, she knew who stood outside the door: *King*.

She slid off the stool, hurried through the foyer, and flung the front door open. King stood on her porch, so ruggedly handsome that her pulse skipped a beat. Furthermore, he was smiling.

"King?"

"You were expecting someone else?" He gathered her into his arms and pressed his lips to her forehead. "Hmm. I've been looking forward to this moment all day. Sorry I'm late."

She pulled away to study his face. "I thought—"

"What?"

He stood straight and tall in the porch light, his boldly handsome features smiling down at her, and in his eyes she saw nothing but affection and weariness.

Thank heaven he didn't know what she'd been thinking. She felt a blush stain her cheeks as she stepped back to let him enter. "Come on in. You look exhausted."

"I am."

"Rough day?"

"A marathon. Started off with David at the university; then I spent all afternoon trying to corral this one high school kid who's being scouted by the majors. The kid wouldn't talk to me without his coach present, and the coach gave me the runaround; then he insisted that I talk to the kid's father first. To make matters worse, I forgot to charge my cell phone, which meant I couldn't get ahold of anyone when I needed them." His gaze came to rest on her questioning eyes. "I've felt hamstrung all day."

Peyton made soft tsking sounds. "Poor baby. Come on, I'll get you some coffee."

"I'm good. Actually, I'd just like to sit and look at you for a while."

Something within her melted under the tenderness of his expression. Forgetting her steely resolutions, she led him into the kitchen. "Did you eat?"

"Grabbed a sandwich on my way to the kid's house." King's eyes widened at the sight of the papers scattered over the counter. "What's all this?"

Peyton settled into her chair. "Background research."

"On?"

"Eve Miller."

He squinted in puzzlement, then snapped his fingers. "The woman who wrote the caustic letter. You called her?"

"I went to see her."

He grinned. "Did she change your mind about being overly cautious?"

"Not yet, she hasn't. But that reminds me—I need to hear your side of the conversation with David."

The furrows in King's forehead deepened as he sank onto the closest barstool. "What do you mean, my side?"

"I've already heard *his* side. He was here, furious, when I got home from work. He said I'd betrayed his trust. Said you yelled at him about his work ethic."

"What work ethic? The kid doesn't have one!"

Peyton groaned as another memory surfaced. "By the way, how'd you find out he'd been cut from the team? I know I didn't tell you."

"His coach and I had breakfast this morning." King crossed his arms. "Why didn't you tell me about David? Didn't you think I might need to know?"

"I thought David should tell you himself, but it sounds like you didn't give him a chance."

"To say what? That he'd 'lost interest'?"

"To explain *why* he lost interest. Did he tell you about art school?"

King laughed, his eyes widening in honest surprise. "Art school? Spare me. One of his buddies probably told him he'd get to draw naked women. I mean, c'mon, the kid couldn't paint a house, let alone a picture."

"That's not the point."

"Isn't it?"

"King—" Peyton broke off as the phone rang. King looked at her, waiting, but Peyton waved the interruption away. "Let the machine get it. It's probably a sales call."

After the beep, the kitchen filled with the sound of a familiar voice. "Um, hi, it's Christine. Listen, I'm gonna have to postpone cleaning out my dad's closet with you tomorrow morning. I'm kinda busy with some other stuff. To be honest, I'm not sure I'm really ready for that. Anyway—" she released a brittle laugh— "I'm sure you're out with King, so I guess we'll talk whenever."

As the phone clicked off, King narrowed his eyes. "They can't communicate," he said, his tone wry, "but they sure can manipulate."

Peyton exhaled in frustration. "If that's what she's doing, then I have to wonder why she needs to. I'm just not good at this, King; I don't know how to handle being a mother, let alone a *step*mother—"

"You're smart; you'll learn like the rest of us—through trial and error." He reached out and gently took her hands. "So you've got Christine's insecurities to deal with, and I've got my failure to communicate with David."

She smiled back, oddly comforted. "We're a mess, aren't we?"

"They're kids, Peyton. They're trying to grow up in a complicated world. There's always going to be some crisis in their lives. We can either deal with them together, or we can use them as an excuse to keep us apart."

Peyton's throat constricted. "You . . . you think I haven't accepted your proposal because I'm looking for an excuse?"

"I think—" King's eyes softened—"that commitment can be terrifying. Especially to someone who's already suffered a loss. But as to whether or not you're looking for an excuse . . . maybe that's a question you need to ask yourself."

Was she? Of course not. He was only looking for ways to convince her that she should say yes, she'd marry him.

She tried to lose herself in his gaze, to rest in his confidence, but iron bands of doubt restrained her heart. She was not good enough for him; she'd never be good enough. He was quick and funny and bright; he ran with his impulses and laughed when things didn't work out as he'd planned. She was plodding and cautious and wary; she made careful decisions and wept bitterly over her mistakes. She loved and admired the man who held her hands, but she'd only make him miserable if she married him.

She closed her eyes, unable to return the unqualified devotion and trust she saw on his face.

After a moment, a perceptible chill rippled through the air. "Listen," King said, his voice flatter now, "I'm going to make it an early night, okay? I'm too tired to be good company."

Too full for words, she could only nod.

He stood and gave her a chaste peck on the forehead, then turned and moved through the foyer. She heard the click of the front door latch, the scrape of his shoes on the steps, and finally the roar of his car as it pulled away.

Peyton stared at the papers on her kitchen counter, then shifted her gaze to the flickering candle in the window. After all, she had lit it only for the fragrance.

Seven

PEYTON CLIMBED UP onto her bed, crossed her legs, and settled her laptop on her knees, relishing the warmth of the machine through her cotton pajamas. After swallowing her initial disappointment at King's early departure, she decided to assuage her depression in the usual way—she'd go to work.

She usually wrote her Monday column on Saturday, but why not get a head start? She could write about baseball and spring training, the advent of spring fever among college students, or the overabundance of newborn puppies and kittens at the local animal shelter. It was still too early to write about St. Patrick, but surely she could come up with something interesting and relevant to her audience.

People loved puppies. She could write about the importance of neutering and spaying pets. Tomorrow she could run down to the ASPCA and take a couple of shots of big-eyed, adorable pups.

She typed her byline and a heading, then tapped her fingertips on the keyboard as she searched for an appropriate lead. Should she open with a personal story? She didn't own a dog now, but she'd had one as a child. Her father liked cocker spaniels, and they'd had a little black cocker named Cinder . . . who died not long after her mother passed away. Her dad always said the dog died of a broken heart.

Peyton swallowed the lump in her throat and wrapped her arms around herself. This wasn't working. Her thoughts were still gloomily colored with the memory of King's stressed face, and she'd never be able to write a decent column until she cleared her head.

The best way to do that was to start typing. Years before, her therapist had taught her that because she was a "word person," writing could unlock the pent-up feelings she had trouble identifying. He gave her a journal and advised her to fill it, which she did, writing page after page each morning. That journal had long been filed away, but she frequently resorted to the exercise, often typing out letters, articles, and diary entries she never meant to be read by anyone.

A grim smile twisted the corner of her mouth as words overflowed her heart and spilled onto the computer screen.

Dear Readers:

I've been feeling like a giant rubber band these days, stretched between responsibilities and loved ones. A year ago, I had few people in my life—just coworkers, friends at church, neighbors I knew only well enough to greet with a smile and a wave.

And then a daughter entered my life, and a man—one of the kindest and most gentle men I have ever known. I love them both and am so grateful that God has brought them into my life, but how do I balance the person I was with the person they want me to be?

My daughter expects me to be a mother—and I am committed to the attempt. I don't know what I'm doing, but I've heard that parenting is a learn-as-you-go enterprise.

The man—he expects me to be a wife, and this is where I find myself balking. If I can scarcely keep my head above water maintaining two close relationships, how am I supposed to handle the intimacy of marriage? Of one thing I am certain—I would rather not try than try and fail. I've seen too much bitterness, met too many people who have been crushed by marital catastrophe.

My mind tells me that I should be cautious; to those who need me, I should parcel myself out in small doses. My heart yearns to make my loved ones happy, but I've unbridled my feelings before with disastrous results.

Peyton stopped typing and looked across the room to a silver framed wedding photo on the top of her bureau. The picture featured her and Gil on their wedding day, fresh-faced and cheek-to-cheek, beaming and in love. A perfect moment, crystallized in time.

She bit her lip, blinked a sudden rush of tears away, and refocused on her computer.

I suppose my quandary boils down to this: in a world in which we must juggle the complex problems of work and family—with all its contemporary definitions—when is the right time to take a chance on love?

That question haunts me these days, nagging me from the time I get out of bed until I close my eyes to sleep.

Why should we risk upsetting the delicate balance we have struggled to achieve in our circumstances? If you have endured the searing grief of loss, for instance, and you finally move from denial, anger, bargaining, and depression into acceptance, wouldn't it be wise to stop and consider the inherent risk before subjecting your heart to the emotional roller coaster of a new and more intimate relationship?

Love is wonderful, but so is friendship. I'm afraid that marrying a beloved male friend is like buying a piece of art you've admired in a mail-order catalog. You may love it when it arrives, but it won't always work with everything else in the house.

What if he doesn't like your taste in furniture? What if he's allergic to your beloved cats? What if conflicts arise between your kid and his kid; whose side do you take?

So many changes; so much to consider. Yes, consider, *as in trusting your brain instead of your heart. Though the fever of hormonal urgency may diminish as we advance in age, our emotions vacillate from one day to the next. How can we know that love won't prove fickle with the passing of time?*

I haven't forgotten what it feels like to be twenty-two

and desperately in love. I can close my eyes and conjure up those giddy heights of joy and pleasure. But I'm no longer twenty-two, and the passing years have added a store of wisdom, however small, to my experience. I keep thinking of a remark I once heard about marriage:

> *"They stood before the altar and supplied*
> *The fire in which their fat was fried."*

I don't want to endure another blazing trial—I've known that particular pain and have no wish to experience it again. Perhaps love is best reserved for the young . . . or for someone more suited to it.

Carl Jung once said, "A man who has not passed through the inferno of his passions has never overcome them."

I have walked through the fire, the ice, and the recovery. So I must regard love with the calm, clear eyes of reason.

Peyton lifted her hands and stared at the words she'd written. There were her feelings, spilled over the page in black-and-white. Her commitment and her confession. Her answer to King, if she could be brave enough to deliver it.

But how should she do that? A man wanted his offer of marriage to be met with excitement and joy, not wariness and doubt. So she'd have to find some way to gently share the news that she couldn't marry him.

She saved the file, closed the lid to her laptop, and set it on the nightstand. She crawled beneath the covers and let a sigh pass through her, an exhalation of weariness that ended only when her eyelids closed.

Peyton reached up and turned out the lamp. She still had to write a column for Monday. But writing this one, at least, had cleared her head so she should be able to sleep.

Eight

CERTAIN THAT CHRISTINE might want to tackle that closet clean-out after all, Peyton rose early on Saturday morning and drove to the home her daughter had shared with her father before the crash of PanWorld flight 848. Wide, treelined streets led to the sprawling colonial, and Peyton felt her heart lift at the sight of the wide lawns and well-maintained homes in the unabashedly suburban neighborhood.

Her daughter had grown up with a nice family, good people. Her adoptive parents had loved her dearly, taken her to church, and encouraged her interest in music. The Lugar family had given Christine a comfortable childhood, a good education, and more cousins than the girl could count. They had provided more than Peyton would have been able to give during those years—so why did she still feel guilty about surrendering her baby?

King would say she was senselessly beating herself up, and her pastor would say she was revisiting matters that had been forgiven long ago. Maybe it wasn't guilt she was feeling; maybe it was regret . . . and perhaps she would always feel it. After all, at some point didn't every woman look back over her life and wish she'd done things differently?

Peyton drew a deep breath and determined to put the past away. For this morning, at least, she would not look back. Today was about looking forward, about helping Christine pack up the past and focus on her future.

She slowed as she neared the redbrick house, then frowned when she saw an unfamiliar van in the driveway. Christine had visitors at 9 a.m.? Maybe a friend had stopped by to pick something up.

She parked on the street, got out of the car, and strolled toward the house, pausing to discreetly place her hand on the hood of the beat-up vehicle. The engine was cold, so the van had been parked here awhile. Christine's car was undoubtedly in the garage, so this driver had arrived after Christine came home from work last night. . . .

A girlfriend, Peyton told herself. Christine was bound to have old high school friends dropping by, or maybe a college-age girlfriend had come to visit over spring break.

When the front door squeaked and opened, she stepped away from the van and then stood in stunned silence as Mike the Tattooed Wonder walked out, a blue recycling bin propped on one hip. He closed the door, hefted the bin into both arms, and stepped over a low-growing shrub as he trudged head down across the lawn, his eyes hidden by scruffy bangs. After dropping the bin at the curb, he turned and moved toward the van, finally lifting his gaze and spotting Peyton.

"Oh. Hi." He spoke in a flat voice and looked at Peyton with cloudy eyes. He showed his teeth in an expression that was more grimace than smile, then walked to the driver's door of the van.

Peyton stepped away as he climbed in, started the engine, and backed out of the driveway. Unappealing images competed with each other for space in her brain—mental pictures of Christine in those tattooed arms, Mike drunkenly kissing the girl's neck . . .

She shook the images away and marched toward the curb. Stopping a few feet away from the mailbox, she was able to see that the recycling bin was filled with empty beer bottles, though Christine wasn't of legal drinking age.

Her thoughts crystallized as her heart pumped anxiety and outrage through her veins. She'd come here as a compassionate friend, but *this* . . . surely this should require a return to "mother" mode.

She strode up the sidewalk, knocked on the door, and tried the doorknob. Unlocked, of course. Which meant any pervert on the street could walk in and help himself to her daughter . . . if one already hadn't.

She opened the door and stepped into the foyer. "Christine?"

"Mom?"

Was that surprise in her voice? Peyton crossed her arms. "Who else?"

"I'm in here."

She followed the voice into the kitchen and found Christine working her way through a pile of dirty dishes by the sink. Peyton crinkled her nose as she surveyed the island countertop covered with spilled salsa, broken tortilla shells, and crumbled ground beef. The place stank of stale beer, and someone had managed to smear avocado dip on the side of the refrigerator.

Peyton couldn't keep a stern note from her voice. "Early morning or late night?"

Christine, bleary-eyed, glanced up from the dishes. "Didn't you get my message?"

"I did. I tried to call you back, several times, but you never answered. Maybe the music was too loud to hear the phone."

Christine dropped a stack of plates into the soapy water. "Probably. I had a few friends over."

Peyton crossed her arms and leaned against the kitchen island. "I saw one of them leaving. The guy who isn't your boyfriend."

Christine looked up again, her gaze sharper this time. "What is *wrong* with you?"

Peyton's breath burned in her throat. "You! Drinking and partying—"

"Drinking and *partying*?"

"—all night, with someone who's way too old for you. *That's* what's wrong with me." Peyton waved at the clutter on every surface. "Is *this* the stuff you were so busy with? So busy you had to cancel our meeting this morning?"

"So what if it *is*?"

Peyton gripped the edge of the counter and struggled to maintain control of her seesawing emotions. Christine had never taken that tone with her, had never sounded so bitter. What was wrong with them? What had happened to her? Peyton had always been a relatively patient person, calm and even-tempered, but the sight of those beer bottles had spurred a reaction she'd never experienced before.

Could it be because she'd never *cared* like this before?

She closed her eyes, took a deep breath, and forced herself to calm down. "Look—" she lowered her voice to a more reasonable pitch—"your father left you this house and all the responsibilities that go with it. Responsibilities you never wanted and shouldn't have been stuck with. And I think you're ticked off about it. I also think you're acting out in ways that are self-destructive—maybe to get even with him."

Christine pulled her arms from the sink and propped them, wet and dripping, on her hips. A thunderous scowl lowered her brow. "That is totally insane."

"Is it?"

"Yes, it is! I don't even drink!"

Peyton snorted. "Right. Mr. Tattoo drank a couple of cases of beer by himself."

Christine rolled her eyes. "He was here with his band. They're cutting a demo and I let them rehearse in my basement. It wasn't a party. They were working, so I made them some food, okay? They're friends. They're talented and I'm going to help them in any way I can."

Peyton felt a whoosh of air go out of her lungs. "A band?"

Christine kept sputtering, rancor sharpening her voice. "As far as being mad at my dad, yeah, you're right. I'm ticked, all right, but not just at him. I'm mad at my adopted mother, who died, too. And at my birth father, who died before I was born. And at you, who actually had a say in the matter and *still* chose to give me away!"

Peyton winced.

"And now," Christine finished, her face flushing to crimson, "if you're finished judging me, I'm running late and I have things to do."

She pushed past Peyton and flew up the stairs, leaving the mess in the kitchen. Peyton leaned on the counter, steeling herself as a tremble rose from someplace deep within her. She'd blown it this time, but surely she had options. She could run upstairs and beg until Christine let her apologize and hug the anger away. Or she could stay here and clean up the kitchen, funneling her emotions into constructive activity.

But this was Christine's house, her kitchen. If Peyton started cleaning, Christine might see her action as interference . . . and more judgment.

Another option remained: she could go home. She could get in the car and drive away, ignoring her mistake and Christine's reaction. The next time they met, maybe neither of them would mention this disastrous encounter.

Peyton walked out of the kitchen and made it as far as the foyer before she realized that running away solved nothing. She'd spent a lifetime running from the past, and what had the effort brought her? Nothing but regrets.

She couldn't walk away this time. She had promised to be around for Christine, and mothers didn't walk away when they hit a bad patch. Some people might give up on their kids, but she had promised to love Christine forever. She couldn't leave.

She turned, her gaze falling on a family portrait on the wall. A pair of too-big front teeth dominated Christine's smile, so she must have been eight or nine when the photo was taken. She wore her dark hair in pigtails and her face was fuller, but the baby Peyton had surrendered was still evident—the big brown eyes had come from Gil, the pointed chin from Peyton.

Her gaze shifted to the woman who had volunteered to raise her daughter. Martha Lugar had been fair and blonde, her nose dusted with a sprinkling of freckles. In the photo, one of her hands was entwined with Christine's, and Peyton felt her heart twist with ruefulness at this evidence of their connection.

Jerry Lugar had been a big, strapping man—a virtual teddy bear. Peyton smiled, immediately understanding why Christine had loved him. The photographer had asked him to kneel on one knee, and despite the awkward pose, his smile appeared warm and genuine. All three Lugars were dressed in blue jeans and white cotton shirts, a far cry from the formal portraits most families favored.

Peyton closed her eyes and breathed a silent prayer of gratitude. She had done the right thing, made the right decision for her baby girl. Christine had been loved and adored.

She always would be.

Almost without meaning to, Peyton climbed the stairs, following a row of family photographs on the wall. She moved down the line, smiling at the evidence of passing years. The sound of running water came from behind a closed door, certainly a bathroom, and Peyton moved silently past it, drinking in details she'd never had the opportunity to ask about.

The trail of memories ended at a large bedroom that must have been Jerry Lugar's. Several extra-large garbage bags sat on the carpet, bulging with what appeared to be sweaters, slacks, and other articles of clothing.

Evidence of the great closet clean-out. The job Christine hadn't been able to finish.

Though she couldn't help feeling that she was trespassing, Peyton moved to the dresser, where several framed photos stood beside a small jewelry box. She was smiling at a picture of a gap-toothed Christine when she heard the squeak of a door hinge and realized the shower was no longer running.

She turned just enough to see Christine standing in the doorway; then she reached out to caress a small framed picture. "Were you embarrassed by those braces?"

Christine didn't answer, but Peyton was in no hurry. She moved to the next photo. "Did you eat as many Girl Scout cookies as you sold? Were you scared on your first day of kindergarten? Did you like to camp out in your backyard? Who gave you your first kiss?" She turned to face her daughter. "Did he break your heart, or did you break his?"

Christine stood in the doorway, wrapped in her robe, her wet hair rippling over her shoulders in black ribbons. Her chin quivered as she stared at the floor.

Peyton pushed past the lump in her throat and found her voice. "I don't know the answer to those and a thousand other questions. I missed so much of your life, Christine. Too much, maybe." A tear slipped from her lower lashes and slid down her cheek. "Because now that I have a chance to be the mother I always dreamed of being, I'm making a total mess of things."

Christine lifted her gaze, her chin still quivering. "All that matters to me," she whispered, "is that you never stop trying."

In a rush of gratitude, Peyton stepped forward to take her daughter into her arms. "Unfortunately, that's about all I can guarantee."

Nine

PEYTON SAT AT the downtown traffic light and wondered if Nora would come for her head before or after lunch.

After her emotional Saturday with Christine, she'd been too spent to think about writing her column for Monday. So on Sunday she crawled out of bed and went to the early church service, praying for inspiration. The pastor chose 1 John 4:16 as his text: "We know how much God loves us, and we have put our trust in his love. God is love, and all who live in love live in God, and God lives in them."

"When we have confidence in the Beloved," the pastor said, his words conjuring up images of King, "we have no fear in love or in life. While we cannot love as perfectly as God does in our own strength, we can allow His love to flow through us."

Peyton squirmed on the pew. She ought to have every confidence in King; the man was as constant as the North Star. But people changed; situations changed. Knowing that, it seemed a miracle that *anyone* was able to get married and stay married.

After a quick lunch, she had come home and riffled through her files, finally finding a partial outline for a column about Middleborough's role in the Civil War. The finished piece was only slightly more interesting than watching paint dry, but the ladies down at the historical society would love it.

Now she glanced out the window and spied a newspaper vending machine at the corner. She already knew what Nora would say about today's column. She would say Peyton was slipping back into her old habits, reporting instead of engaging. The Heart Healer was supposed to evoke readers' emotions, not report facts about places and events that had little to do with today's world.

But yesterday Nora had no choice; she either had to run Peyton's lousy column or come up with something to fill the space. She would have opted for running the historical piece and penciling in a stern talk with the Heart Healer for Monday. Morning or afternoon?

A car behind Peyton honked, yanking her from her thoughts. She glanced up, saw that the light had changed, and drove through the intersection.

Her cell phone rang, distracting her from the traffic. Peyton pressed the button for her hands-free control. "Hello?"

"Hey." King's voice filled the car with warmth. "Good weekend?"

Peyton's mood shifted from anxiety to euphoria. They hadn't parted on the best of terms and he hadn't called over the weekend. She'd tried not to worry, tried to focus on Christine and her work, but it hadn't been easy.

Now here he was, sounding confident and steady and strong.

"It was a good weekend. Spent all day Saturday with Christine and whipped out a column yesterday."

"Haven't had a chance to read it yet."

"I wouldn't rush—unless you have a burning interest in Middleborough's contributions to the Confederate Army."

He laughed. "Sorry I didn't get to see you, but I was setting up some things for my trip. I'm on my way to the airport for my interview in New York. Can I see you when I get back?"

She gripped the steering wheel as her pulse rate increased. He was making an appointment, sounding official. Which might mean that tonight he'd press her for an answer to the question that had been hanging over their heads for five days. "You'll be back tonight?"

"Unless something unexpected comes up. My flight's scheduled to land at six."

She felt her stomach sway but forced a bright note into her voice. "Okay, sure. I'll pick up Italian."

"Sounds like a plan. See you soon."

She powered the phone off, then pulled into the *Times* parking lot. Most of the spaces were already filled, which meant she was running late. Nora didn't like it when her writers straggled into the daily news budget meeting after nine o'clock, even if they did manage to file their assignments on time.

Peyton grabbed her laptop, locked the car, and hurried toward the front door. The security guard greeted her with a nod and a salute, then bent his finger in a come-here gesture.

She halted in the hallway. "What?"

The guard took a half step toward her. "Marry the guy," he called in a stage whisper. "Don't keep us in suspense."

Peyton forced a distracted smile and walked away, her thoughts whirling. How did the security guard hear about her and King? He could have seen them leaving the building together, or maybe he'd heard about those kisses stolen on office time. Maybe King had shown him the ring or asked his opinion. One never knew with a man friendly enough to talk to a fence post.

She took the elevator up to the second floor and stepped into a hubbub of activity. Nora was standing in the lobby, one hand on her hip, her gaze focused on the clock as the members of her staff grabbed cups of coffee and strolled toward the conference room.

"I'm coming," Peyton said, waving as she passed the editor. "I got held up in traffic."

"By the way—" Nora caught Peyton's sleeve, then indulged in a reluctant smile—"nice job on the column today. You should be that transparent more often."

Peyton froze, staring, as her arms pebbled with gooseflesh. Her latest column wasn't transparent at all. At least it *shouldn't* have been.

"Excuse me." She yanked her sleeve from Nora's grasp and hurried back to the elevator, sliding through the exiting crowd like water.

"Peyton? Are you all right?"

Ignoring the editor's call, Peyton ducked into the car and jabbed at the button for the ground floor, then stood against the stainless steel wall, her toe tapping, until the elevator groaned

Peyton ponders a note from Eve Miller, one of her column readers.

Christine Lugar is the daughter Peyton gave up for adoption nineteen years ago.

Kingston Danville, senior sports editor, works with Peyton at the newspaper.

Peyton asks Mandi to research Eve Miller's past.

Peyton and King share an affectionate moment in the office.

Peyton and King read the letter from Eve Miller.

King asks Peyton to marry him.

Peyton and David discuss his falling-out with his father.

Peyton and King consider complications challenging their relationship.

Peyton and Christine adjust to their new mother-daughter relationship.

Mandi and Peyton discuss Peyton's visit with Eve.

Young Eve accepts a challenge from a young Ben Morrick.

Mandi gives Peyton Ben Morrick's address.

King listens as Peyton gives him his son's new work address.

Peyton shares her vulnerability with King.

Father and son bond after King discovers David's artistic talent.

Peyton writes a column about Eve and her decision to take the "well-marked path" forty years ago.

Eve and Ben: A reunion forty years in the making.

Together Peyton and King exchange vows and commit their lives to each other.

Peyton gazes at King as he commits his love to her.

King looks on lovingly as Peyton says, "I do."

King slips the wedding band on Peyton's finger.

Peyton and King savor the joy after saying, "I do."

Peyton and King greet well-wishers outside the church after the ceremony.

Peyton and King are surrounded by cheering family and friends.

Peyton throws her bouquet high above the joyous crowd.

and took her back to the first floor. She bit her tongue, waiting impatiently for the doors to open; then she fought the incoming crowd to reach the stack of freshly printed papers on a vestibule table.

She picked up a paper, fumbled to the second section, and scanned the left side of the page. Beneath her customary byline, she saw the words she'd been dreading: *I've been feeling like a giant rubber band these days, stretched between responsibilities and loved ones.*

"No." She lowered the paper as blood pounded thickly in her ears. What had she done? She must have pressed Send when she finished the column she wrote Saturday night for her own eyes only. Her wireless network would have sent the piece winging to Nora's in-box before Peyton even closed the laptop lid.

She stumbled down the hallway and leaned against the polished wooden wall, feeling as though her bones had turned to ash. The newspaper in her hand fluttered to the floor. King would read this. Maybe this morning on the way to New York. He'd settle into his seat, pull out the local section, and smile, eager to see the column she'd jokingly disparaged. Then he'd read her most honest thoughts, the thoughts she'd never wanted anyone else to see.

After reading them, what would stop him from accepting the *Times*'s offer?

Later, Peyton would barely remember the staff meeting. She sat at the table in a paralysis of disbelief, only dimly aware of the whispers and curious smiles cast in her direction. When the meeting broke up, she went straight to her desk, waved away Mandi's concerned questions, and dropped her head into her hands.

When she finally worked up enough courage, she picked up the newspaper and read her column again, trying to see the words with King's eyes. *That question haunts me these days, nagging me. . . . I don't want to endure another blazing trial—I've known that particular pain and have no wish to experience it again. Perhaps love is best reserved for the young . . . or for someone more suited to it.*

She groaned as a cold lump grew in her stomach. King would not understand. She couldn't have hurt him more if she'd thrust a knife between his ribs and turned the handle. Not only had she written a refusal to his proposal, she had declared her answer to the world before sharing it with him.

She was occupying her chair like a hopeless sack of skin when Nora stopped by her desk. "What's wrong?" the editor asked, her brow furrowing. "I've never seen you get upset about budget cuts."

"I'm not upset about the budget cuts." Peyton's voice came out as a croak. "I'm upset about my column."

"I liked it. Your readers are going to identify with all of those confused emotions."

"I'm not worried about my readers. I'm worried about King."

The editor's face twisted with a small grimace, as if she'd considered King's reaction for the first time. "Haven't you discussed all this with him?"

"Not yet. I was still sorting through my feelings."

"So why'd you write it?"

"I didn't mean to publish it. I wrote it . . . as a sort of exercise. I must have sent it to you without thinking. I meant for you to run the historical piece today."

"Oh, that." Nora sniffed. "That one could use some work. I was going to suggest that you take another look at it."

"Oh." Peyton sighed, not surprised. "Of course."

"Hey, don't worry about it." Nora smiled and clicked her fingernails on the edge of Peyton's desk. "King will understand. Maybe he'll even get a laugh out of your slipup."

Peyton shook her head. "I don't think so."

"But what's done is done and it sounds like you've made your decision. So get to work; get out of the office; get on with your life. Get on with that anniversary feature—I need it by Friday."

Peyton propped her head on her hand and groaned. "Thanks for the reminder."

Like she needed one.

❧

Half an hour later she had shelved her unruly emotions and was back in her car, turning onto the street that would take her to Eve Miller's house. The woman hadn't wanted to talk without learning about Peyton's personal life; well, if she read the paper, she was now an expert. Maybe she'd be willing to talk today.

In the sunlight the narrow lane was prettier than Peyton remembered, the bare shrubbery dotted with yellow green buds and young leaves. She parked across the street from the Miller home, then pulled her collar closer to her throat as she walked up to the front door. She had asked Mandi to call with the news that Peyton was on her way, but she had a feeling Eve Miller wouldn't require advance notice. The woman seemed unflappable.

Peyton knocked, and a moment later Eve opened the door. Today she wore a mud-spattered apron over a smock and blue jeans, so apparently she'd been working. The shadow of irritation in her eyes vanished when she recognized Peyton. "Ah! So you made it after all."

"Did my assistant reach you?"

"No, but I don't mind impromptu visits." She leaned against the doorframe and smiled in patient amusement. "Have you reconsidered my terms, Ms. MacGruder?"

"Peyton, please. And yes, I'd like to have a *conversation*, if you're still willing."

"I am indeed. Come in, please."

Peyton stepped into the studio. A fire crackled in the fireplace, warding off the chill, and a cup of tea sat on the small desk.

"Have a seat, please." Eve moved to the kettle and filled a second cup. "So . . . what brought you back?"

Peyton sat on the edge of a small chair and searched for the right words. "I'm sort of at a crossroads myself right now. In my personal life."

An easy smile played at the corners of Eve's mouth. "I thought it might be something like that. I read your column this morning."

"I thought you might have." Peyton shook her head as she accepted the steaming cup. "That column was a mistake. I meant to write it, but I didn't mean to publish it."

Eve lifted her own teacup and curled up on the sofa. "Maybe you did. Sometimes the unconscious mind knows exactly what it is doing."

Peyton snorted. "I hardly think I'm determined to sabotage one of the best relationships I've ever known. But I didn't come here to whine about my situation. I came because I'm on deadline and I really want to hear your story."

"I'm glad." Eve sipped from her cup while Peyton inhaled the scent of the aromatic liquid; then the older woman set her cup on a table. "Now that you're here, Peyton, let's put our cards on the table. Can I assume you did some research on me?"

Peyton felt her cheeks flush with warmth. "Well . . ."

"You'd be a lousy reporter if you hadn't. What did you learn?"

Grateful that the woman was finally willing to cooperate, Peyton set down her cup and pulled her steno pad from her purse. "Both you and your husband came from well-to-do, politically connected families."

Eve nodded. "Our mothers were sorority sisters. Billy and I were destined to be together—at least in our mothers' minds—from the time we were conceived."

"You studied art at Davidson—"

"Right. Of course my father assumed I'd never be able to earn a living selling my work. He insisted that I earn a teaching credential." She transferred her gaze to the picture of her husband and his friends on the desk. "Which brings us to that photograph you noticed and the beginning of the story I want to tell you. By the way, do you take milk with your tea?"

Peyton shook her head. "I'm fine, thanks."

Eve turned her attention back to the photo. "Billy joined the Navy after he graduated from Duke. By the time he entered flight school, we were engaged. At his urging, I followed him to Newport News, where I found a job teaching at a private girls' school near the base."

"How old were you then?"

Eve closed her eyes and smiled. "Twenty-four. So very young."

Peyton sipped her tea, thinking of eighteen-year-old Christine.

"Billy had become quite close to the guys in his training crew," Eve continued. "When I showed up, they graciously accepted me as the fourth musketeer."

"So you all hung out together?"

"When they weren't training, we were inseparable."

Peyton reached for her pen. "Tell me about them."

"With pleasure." Eve released a throaty laugh. "Richie was full of joy and life. Delighted by every breath God gave him."

"Are you still in touch with him?"

"Was, until he died. Several years back, from cancer."

Peyton's gaze shifted to the other young man in the picture. "And the pilot?"

"Ben Morrick." Eve smiled but with a distracted look, as though she were listening to something only she could hear. "Ben was the direct opposite of Billy. From the south side of Chicago, tough and street smart. Charming, though. He loved speed and danger. He crashed twice during their training, and both times I wanted to wring his neck. He was always taking stupid chances. Billy saved his bacon the second time, pulled him out of burning wreckage."

Peyton made a note on her steno pad. "Sounds like a real daredevil."

"I think he just wanted to get all he could out of life. He was always trying to get the rest of us to join him in one crazy stunt or another."

"Such as?"

Memory softened Eve's eyes and a recollection tightened the corner of her mouth. "There was this one crispy cold day a few weeks before they were to ship out. We all decided to go for a hike in the woods not far from the base. . . ."

Ten

"HEY! WAIT UP!"

Billy's cry echoed among the golden poplars and the pines. He and Richie were bringing up the rear, but Eve was determined to keep up with Ben, who had led the way into the glorious autumn woods. He left the trail and went zigzagging between the trees, loping over the carpet of fallen leaves as confidently as a deer.

"Ben Morrick!" she called, a note of exasperation in her voice. "Wait up!"

Billy's and Richie's cries grew fainter as she broke into a run. Her mother would have a fit if she knew her daughter was sprinting through the Virginia woods like some kind of rustic, but it felt good to stretch her legs and fly. To leave her classroom and the base behind, to outrun responsibility and obligation and the expectations that hovered over her like a thundercloud.

"Ben?" Eve rounded an overgrown evergreen and peered through the woods, but she could no longer see the khaki blur of his uniform. "If you're planning to jump out and scare me, Ben, you can just forget that idea. You know I hate surprises. So come on out and let me see you."

She stopped and listened intently but heard nothing except the whisper of the wind and the distant gurgle of running water. Maybe she'd fallen farther behind than she realized. If a stream lay ahead, Ben might already be there, waiting and wondering what had happened to her.

She ran again, not caring about the branches that whipped her skirt and snagged her sweater. Thank goodness the chilly weather had sent the bugs and spiders into hiding. The ground slanted ahead of her, a slope led away from the trail toward whatever lay at the bottom of this hill, but she ran on, her heart pounding with every step. Too late, she saw the fallen log; too abruptly she tried to leap over it. She might have made it un-scathed, but the sole of her loafer slipped on the damp autumn leaves. Down she went, landing in an undignified heap at the base of a sycamore.

She had barely brushed the leaves from her hair before Ben arrived, breathless and agitated. He bent over her, his eyes dark with worry. "Eve? My goodness, are you all right? I shouldn't have, I didn't mean—"

"I'm fine." Irritated and embarrassed, she spat the words at him. "Stop your mollycoddling and help me up."

His hand clasped hers and pulled her to her feet. She relaxed her fingers, certain that he would release her as soon as she'd found her balance, but he kept his hand wrapped around hers as he led her up the sloping hill. "I'm a darned fool," he muttered under his breath. "Shouldn't have led you off the trail, but I never dreamed you'd follow. Billy's going to kill me."

She stopped, forcing him to look at her in the silent woods. "Don't—" her eyes met his—"worry about Billy. I took off after you and it's my fault I fell."

"But I shouldn't have—"

"I could keep up with you anywhere, Ben Morrick." She gentled her voice as she studied him and hoped the longing apparent in his face was not quite so obvious in her own. "Anytime, anyplace."

Neither of them spoke as the silence filled with a wind whistling down the slope. Ben automatically stepped closer, sheltering her from the chilly breeze. She lifted her hands to his arms, aware of the delicate thread that had begun to form between them, and he stared at her as if he were committing her face to memory.

He looked away when Billy's voice rang out in the stillness.

"Ben? You seen my girl?"

"Here!" Ben called, his jaw flexing. "She's here."

He led her back to the trail, keeping her hand safe in his, but he released her when Billy and Richie came around the curve. Because her hand felt cold and naked without Ben's, Eve thrust her hands into her pockets.

Richie's bold laugh echoed among the trees, and Billy winked at Eve as he strode past her. "Why'd you slow down? Did y'all get tired?"

"No." Eve glanced at Ben. "I don't feel tired at all."

The four of them followed the path until they reached a

rustic footbridge that crossed a deep ravine. Beneath it, probably twenty feet down, a mountain stream gurgled over rocks and dead leaves. Billy stood on the bridge and threw stones into the foaming water, then leaned against the railing and closed his eyes. Richie pulled out his binoculars and studied the treetops for birds.

Ben climbed onto the narrow railing.

As he teetered on the narrow beam, Eve took a deep, quivering breath to calm the racing pulse beneath her rib cage. "Ben Morrick, you climb down from there."

"Nah." He grinned at her. "I can see better from up here."

"See what?" Billy opened one eye and squinted up at his friend. "You can't see anything up there that we can't see down here."

"Maybe," Ben answered, "but I'm getting a rush you'll never know, tenderfoot."

Eve crossed her arms. It wasn't fair. They got to fly, they got to travel, and all she got was a classroom of bored students. She would never know real fear, real excitement, unless . . .

She stepped forward and gripped the railing. "I want to see."

"Evie." Billy's voice was dour and disapproving. "Don't even joke about it."

"I'm not joking." Before he could pull her from the rail, Eve stepped onto the lower plank and threw one leg over the railing. Sitting astride the beam, she held on with both hands and looked at Ben.

"Eve." His voice held a note of uncertainty. "I don't want you to get hurt."

"But you'll help me?"

Indecision flickered in his eyes; then he extended his hand.

Eve reached out and grasped his fingers. Clinging to the strength in his arm—he felt as solid as the bridge—she pulled herself up, planted her feet on the rail, and stood. Richie applauded and whistled, but Billy frowned. "Eve," he ordered, hands on hips, "get down this instant."

"You're not my father," she said, keeping her voice light. Holding tight to Ben's fingers, she took a dancing step toward him.

"Eve!" Billy swore softly and stepped forward as if to grab her.

"Back off," Ben growled. "You don't want to make her lose her balance, do you?"

Billy glowered in response, but he retreated. Eve focused on Ben, not caring what her fiancé thought. Ben was an anchor; with his fingertips alone he guided her, balanced her, somehow completed her. She felt as though she could do a cartwheel on this railing, as long as she could manage to hold on to Ben's hand.

"Girl—" Billy's voice deepened—"if you fall and break your neck, what am I going to tell your parents? You want your father to skin me alive?"

She looked at Ben, saw the hesitation in his eyes. Did she see desire as well?

"Eve," Richie chimed in, "if you don't climb down, Billy's going to be a terror to live with. You ever tried to live with a terror?"

Eve drew a deep breath and smiled into Ben's eyes. "Ready for the dismount?"

"Shall we do a double?"

"You mean—both of us jump at once?"

"Yeah—but let's jump *toward* the bridge. We don't want to give Billy and Richie a heart attack."

Desperate to prolong the magic moment, Eve squeezed Ben's hand; then they turned on the makeshift balance beam and jumped together. They landed safely on the wide planks, hands still linked, to enthusiastic applause . . . from Richie alone.

"Not funny," Billy growled, pulling his shoulders back. "And it's getting late. We'd better go."

Though she hadn't offered it, he took her hand and led her down the path. Ben and Richie followed, and several times on the long walk Eve turned and tried to catch Ben's expression.

But the day was old, and the shadows were long—and deep enough to hide Ben's face.

Eleven

EVE'S VOICE TRAILED away as she finished her story. She stared at nothing as a rueful smile curved her mouth. Was she aware that a glow lit her face every time she spoke of Ben Morrick?

Peyton lowered her teacup. "Were you always a daredevil?"

Eve's face changed, the mask shattering in surprise. "I'd hardly call myself a daredevil. But whenever anyone twirls a red flag in my direction, I do have a tendency to charge it."

Peyton tilted her head and considered the graceful woman before her. Hard to imagine this genteel person climbing fences and running through the woods with three servicemen, but Eve Miller had already proven herself unconventional. "I have a feeling Billy wasn't happy about your balance beam routine on the bridge."

Eve released a delicate snort. "He didn't speak to me for most of a week. At one point, he actually accused Ben of trying to murder his fiancée."

"He must have wondered about your wild streak."

"I wasn't wild, not really—more like repressed. The world in which I grew up did not celebrate nonconformity . . . or diversity. Mama could scarcely believe I counted a black man among my friends."

"Yet Billy came from your world, too."

Eve lifted a brow. "Now you're beginning to understand."

Peyton made a note as the pieces fell into place: a young woman in the sixties, raised according to standards of Southern gentility, befriends her fiancé's brothers-in-service, but one of them is black and the other a Yankee. Her family must have been desperate to see her safely married off to Billy.

She lowered her pen. "Whatever happened to Ben Morrick?"

Eve's face remained perfectly composed as she lifted her teacup. "After he served in Vietnam, he married a Cambodian woman. Stayed in Asia, flying mercy missions for NGOs."

"NGO?"

"Sorry—I tend to forget that civilians don't speak in acronyms. Nongovernmental organizations."

"Sounds like he turned out to be a good guy."

"I suppose."

"So . . . when was the last time you saw him?"

A look passed over Eve's face, a haunted expression Peyton recognized from her own mirror. "We'll have to save that story," she said, glancing at her watch. She gestured to her potter's wheel. "My clay is drying and I need to attend to it."

Peyton set her teacup on the table. "I . . . I've enjoyed this."

"Why don't you bring a couple of sandwiches with you tomorrow? We can talk over lunch. It's your turn, you know, to explain your most recent column . . . and to tell me about Gil."

Peyton froze, her hand on her notebook. "Did I mention my husband's name?"

"We're traveling on a two-way street, remember? I did a bit of research myself. Your husband died in a traffic accident twenty years ago. You were pregnant at the time. You placed the baby for adoption but were reunited with her last Christmas, after the jet crash."

"How—how could you know all that? Did you google—"

"Nothing so obvious." Eve's eyes twinkled. "Snooping is easy when you have a well-placed source. One of the paper's art critics is a friend of mine."

"And a shameless gossip!"

Eve's smile deepened into laughter. "Yes, that too. He also told me you're involved with the sports editor. A man who, I'd be willing to bet, has more than a little to do with the crossroads you mentioned in your column today."

A reluctant grin crept across Peyton's face. Eve Miller might be colorful and outspoken, but she was certainly no fool. "And I thought I was a good investigator. I'd better guard my job."

"Tomorrow, then?"

"I'll be here. With sandwiches." She stood and moved to the door, then hesitated. "Any special kind you like?"

Eve settled on the stool behind her potter's wheel. "Surprise me."

"Please, Lord, don't let King have time to read today's paper."

Peyton murmured that prayer yet again, then pulled the foil

cover from a tray of take-out Italian and inhaled the rich aroma. Her favorite restaurant had risen to the occasion, so at least she wouldn't have to worry that King wouldn't like this dinner. The man was a good sport, usually eating everything she put in front of him, including some meals that were definitely not boyfriend-worthy.

So why couldn't she marry him?

Ignoring the intrusive question, she ran her finger along the edge of the pan, scraped up a fingerful of sauce, and tasted it. Perfect and still warm. Just what a hungry man would want after a long day of airports and meetings.

She moved to the stereo and put on a jazz album that always lifted her spirits. Her mood had improved remarkably after leaving Eve's house; making progress toward a goal always made her feel better. She'd gone back to the office to find her in-box overflowing with e-mails. At least fifty readers were responding to her Sunday column with examples of their own crossroads experiences, and another dozen or so wanted to know more about what was happening in her private life.

She didn't read any of the responses. Too many words, too many opinions, would only cloud her mind and blot out the bright light of hope that passing time had planted in her heart. There was always a chance, however small, that King hadn't picked up a paper, had been too distracted to think about Middleborough, and was planning to come straight from the airport to her house. Tonight she would explain the mistake; she would say she had only meant to play devil's advocate with herself, she had never meant to submit the piece.

And she had never meant to hurt him.

She was washing up when the doorbell rang. The sound sent a tremor scooting up her spine, but as she dried her hands, she looked in the mirror and told herself that King was a reasonable man; he'd understand her mistake. Then she hurried to the front door.

King stood on the porch, his hands in his pockets and circles of fatigue under his eyes. Her heart went out to him. "I hope you like ravioli con funghi," she said, her voice artificially bright. "They were out of that lasagna you like—"

"Listen, Peyton, I'm sorry, but I can't stay."

She pressed her hand to her chest, but the burning rock of guilt beneath her breastbone wasn't going anywhere. "I bought enough food to feed an army—"

King shook his head, his face rippling with anguish. "David's moved out of his dorm and nobody seems to know where he's gone, including his mother. She's been calling me nonstop all day. Panicked. Ticked off. She says it's all my fault that he quit school."

Peyton sagged against the doorframe, simultaneously relieved and saddened. He was upset about David, not her. And if he'd spent all day worrying about David, he probably hadn't had time to read her column.

"On top of that," King continued, "there's this New York thing."

She crossed her arms. "How'd the interview go? Did you charm them?"

A crooked grin flitted across his face. "Must have. They made me an offer on the spot."

"Really?" She forced a smile. "I'm not surprised, Mr. Irresistible."

"To everyone but you, it seems." She felt her smile stiffen as he continued. "They want a five-year commitment and a decision by the end of this week."

She swallowed hard over a suddenly tight throat. "I see."

"It's unlikely, at my age, that I'll get another opportunity like this, Peyton." His use of her first name caught her by surprise, as did the hand that slipped beneath her chin and lifted her gaze to meet his. "I hope you know I'd happily pass it by if you'll just agree to marry me—even though my proposal has *haunted* and *nagged* at you for the last several days."

Peyton felt her stomach drop as the worries that had been lapping at her subconscious crested and crashed. "King, that column was a mistake. I never meant to file it; I was only trying to verbalize my thoughts."

"I realized that, Peyton, and I've had all day to think about what you wrote. About us." He slid his hands into his pockets and smiled, though the smile didn't reach his eyes. "I don't know what you're looking for, but if I can't make you happy, maybe you should just tell me now."

She tried to control herself, but her chin wobbled and her eyes filled in spite of her efforts. "King, you're a wonderful man and I adore you."

"But you're afraid I'll develop an allergy to your cats? Or maybe it's my divorce that's bothering you. Maybe you think I don't know how to stick around for the long haul."

She flinched. Blood pounded in her ears so thickly she could barely hear her own voice as she protested. "Your divorce has nothing to do with my indecision."

"Then what's the problem? If you know your own heart, why can't you say yes?"

He waited, his eyes searching her face, and his mouth twisted when a tear rolled down her cheek. He must have found his answer in that single tear, because he leaned forward, kissed her on the forehead, and walked away.

Peyton stepped back into the house but remained at the door, one hand pressed to the wooden surface, the other supporting her aching head. What was she *doing*? The right thing, the honest thing? Or was she throwing happiness away with both hands?

Twelve

ON TUESDAY, PEYTON beat the morning traffic and arrived at the office before the crowd, filing a column about an animal rescue organization well before her 11:30 deadline.

"Pug Rescue?" Mandi crinkled her nose and waved a hard copy before Peyton's eyes. "Where'd this idea come from?"

"From the desperation file." Peyton rolled her chair out from under her desk. "If Nora doesn't like it—well, too bad. I've got no time to research anything else if she still wants that feature story by Friday."

"What about your reader mail? Your in-box is crammed full of responses from your weekend column. You want me to go through them?"

"You'd be doing me a huge favor if you would." Peyton smiled in relief as she stood and slipped into her jacket. "Thank everyone for writing and pull out any letters that might be worth a second look. And now I have to run; I have a lunch appointment."

Mandi's gaze darted toward King's office. "With him?"

"With Eve Miller. I promised to bring sandwiches." Peyton halted, her steno pad in her hand. "Do you know a deli in the west end of town? Something unconventional, maybe? Eve doesn't seem like the hoagie type."

Mandi grinned. "You want Sweet Sage, at the corner of Main and Fifty-first. It's a sandwich shop for chicks."

"Which means?"

"They serve a lot of quiche and put sprouts on the side of almost every order. And tea—they offer lots of different teas."

"That's the ticket." Peyton grabbed her purse from her bottom drawer and gave Mandi a quick salute. "Thanks. I'll be back later this afternoon."

"Let the clay slide between your palms," Eve encouraged, her voice a soothing murmur in Peyton's ear, "while pressing evenly from both sides. There, that's good; maintain a steady pressure. Urge the bowl's wall to become thinner as your hands glide upward."

Peyton leaned forward and concentrated on the spinning clay between her hands. Throwing a pot looked like child's play when Eve sat at the wheel, but this was Peyton's third attempt to form a simple bowl shape. Her first two misshapen efforts sat off to the side.

"That's good." Eve nodded as Peyton's bowl stretched upward beneath the pressure of her hands. "You're making the shape more delicate, but at the same time—"

Peyton gasped as her bowl began to wobble. An instant later the top portion fell in on itself.

"—more fragile."

Eve smiled as she snapped off the electric motor. "Don't worry. It takes a while to get the hang of it."

Peyton lifted her muddy hands. "I should have stopped while I was ahead—like just before I sat down."

"Don't say that." Eve's voice chided her gently. "No one achieves success without first finding the courage to face potential failure."

"But I've wasted all this clay—"

"You haven't wasted a thing because clay can be reused. I like to think of it as the medium of second chances." Eve walked to the sink and dropped a dish towel into a bowl of warm water. "So— tell me about your sports editor friend. From what I read in your column, your relationship appears to be somewhat serious."

Peyton used the back of her wrist to brush a hank of hair from her eyes, then gratefully accepted the wet towel. "It *was* serious—he proposed last week. I put him off, though, until last night when he pressed me for an answer I couldn't give." She concentrated on wiping the mud from her fingers, then looked up and caught Eve's questioning gaze.

"Couldn't give," Eve asked, "or wouldn't?"

Peyton dropped the towel and pulled off the mud-splashed apron Eve had insisted she wear. "My Monday column didn't help matters any. His proposal should have made me happy. After reading that column, he probably thinks I found the idea of marrying him sheer torture."

"All right then." Eve's voice brightened as she dried her own hands. "Let's talk about something else."

"Like what?"

"Well . . . how about your relationship with Gil?"

Peyton frowned. Did all older women believe they had the right to pry into others' lives? Even though she'd promised to talk about herself, she hadn't agreed to dig up ancient history. "If you don't mind, I'd rather not discuss my late husband. He's not really relevant to my current situation."

"Hey—" Eve's cheek curved in a smile—"you and I made a deal: we would open our lives, like a book. And most people read a book by starting at the beginning."

Peyton crossed her arms and tried to disguise her annoyance. "Okay. Let's make it quick, though."

"Fine. How long were you married before you got pregnant?"

"Two years."

Eve nodded as she carried her newly thrown pot to a shelf. "Was your husband excited about having a baby?"

Peyton braced herself for the painful unlocking of the past. "He'd been my professor in college." She stiffened, momentarily abashed. "It's embarrassing—such a cliché."

"Go on."

"Gil was exactly what you'd expect—handsome, rumpled, charming, and as smart as a whip. He wore his tweed jacket well."

Eve's mouth quirked with humor. "You must have had plenty of competition for his attention."

"Let's just say he did nothing to discourage his popularity— before or after we were married."

A faint line formed between Eve's brows as she gave Peyton a bright-eyed glance. "And fatherhood? How'd he deal with that?"

Peyton grimaced. She hadn't dredged up these memories in years; aside from thinking about Christine, she hadn't wanted to look back. No one could move forward if they spent too much time looking back, and nothing good ever came of dwelling in the past.

Either Eve Miller must consider herself an armchair psychologist or she was a secret sadist. In any case, the lady was persistent, so Peyton might as well throw her a bone.

"He tried to accept the coming baby," she admitted, sinking into a chair by the window. "But fatherhood didn't exactly fit his self-image. Once I started to show, he became more and more . . . I don't know, disengaged."

Eve sat on the sofa and regarded Peyton with a sympathetic smile. "A word I understand very well. *Disengaged* would be the best I could say about my relationship with Billy. Our marriage was, in essence, arranged by our parents and our own expectations. And it proved to be a disaster."

"Because . . . Billy wasn't a good husband?"

"I won't blame him for a fiasco that wasn't entirely his fault. If we'd been better friends, if we'd only met each other halfway, we might have pulled it off. But I couldn't commit to that . . . because I was in love with someone else."

Peyton leaned forward, propping her elbows on her knees. "Let me guess—Ben Morrick."

Eve looked at her for a moment, then broke eye contact, her gaze drifting off to less uncomfortable territory. "Ben and I tried our best—both of us—to not become involved. But it seemed inevitable." She smiled; then her expression shifted to an inward look. Whatever, whenever she was thinking of, she was going there again.

Thirteen

BECAUSE THE BOYS had liberty that Friday night, Eve met them down at Jim's Place, a pool hall not far from the base. A sea of khaki flooded the joint, brightened here and there with the cupcake hues of the local girls in their summer dresses.

Richie, Ben, and Billy ordered their drinks and headed toward the pool tables, eager to place a few wagers and take a turn at the game. Billy kept his hand firmly wrapped around Eve's, but he turned her loose when the winner of a game of eight ball nodded his way and said, "Rack 'em up."

Eve hung back, one arm wrapped around her middle, as Billy racked up the balls and chalked his pool cue. After his opponent broke, he bent across the table to take his first shot, then glanced over his shoulder. "Hey, Ben! Dance with Eve, will ya? She's bored. I can't stand her staring daggers at me."

Billy grinned at her, probably expecting her to protest, but she kept her face composed in an expressionless mask as she turned and walked toward the dance floor. Ben followed behind her, the pressure of his eyes heating the back of her neck like a laser beam. On the dance floor, he took her hand, lifting her spirits with a smile that crinkled the corners of his brown eyes.

Out of habit, she protested. "Ben, you don't have to . . ."

But then she fell silent. She'd been expecting to see resignation on his face or maybe a touch of humor, but the look in his eyes chased the rest of the words right out of her head.

Ben Morrick looked at her with eyes from which the pretense of indifference had been peeled away. He smiled, a trace of unguarded tenderness on his lips, and placed his other hand on her hip. "May I—" his hand tightened on hers—"have this dance?"

Men laughed in a back corner, bottles chinked at the bar, and pool balls cracked on the distant tables, but Eve heard only Ben and Percy Sledge wailing on the jukebox: "When a man loves a woman . . ."

After a moment of swaying in time to the music, Ben dropped her hand and locked both of his hands behind her back, drawing her closer than a man's best friend ought to. But she didn't care, and she doubted Billy would, either, if he ever bothered to look away from his game. Ben led her away from the pool tables, swirling through air thick with the gray haze of spent cigarettes and the twining tendrils of live ones.

When Percy stopped singing, she and Ben stood motionless, locked in each other's arms. Someone dropped in another quarter, and the Association began to sing "Cherish." Eve tightened her grip around Ben's neck and smiled into his eyes until she heard the group sing:

"Perish is the word that more than applies to the hope in my heart each time I realize—"

With a choking cry, she lowered her cheek to Ben's shoulder and felt his arms flex around her in response. What were they doing? Walking the knife-edge of danger, that's what. Risking Billy's anger and her parents' displeasure, risking the destruction of a friendly foursome that had been together for months. Richie might well side with Billy and blame Ben for the breakup. Her parents would have a coronary if she phoned home to announce that she'd fallen in love with a boy from Chicago. Billy's parents would be speechless if she called off the wedding, and of course they'd blame her for ruining their grand plans.

And what of those plans? The wedding date had been set for more than a year, the church reserved, the flowers ordered. Billy's sister, her cousins, the minister, the groomsmen—everyone had already cleared their calendars for what promised to be the wedding of the year.

Eve lifted her head and gazed at Ben, imagining him in a tuxedo and standing before the altar, those brown eyes smiling and waiting for her.

What sort of miracle would it take to change her destiny and make that dream come true?

Fourteen

EVE LOOKED UP, alert and present, but with traces of the past in her eyes. "Billy and I respected each other, but little affection and even less love existed between us. Our life together was destined to be rich in privilege but completely devoid of passion."

Peyton opened her hands. "So . . . if you loved Ben, why did you marry Billy? You weren't so repressed that you were afraid to break free of convention."

"It was a different world back then, a different place." Eve tilted her head as a small smile ruffled her mouth. "Do you love—what's his name? your sports guy?"

"Kingston. *King* . . . and yes, I do love him."

"Yet you can't bring yourself to marry him. Why is that?"

Peyton snorted. "The situations are nothing alike."

"Are you sure about that? Seems to me that we've both been caught up in a definite and passionate love . . . but we ran into problems when it became necessary to turn that love into a commitment."

Peyton stiffened. "I am *not* afraid to commit."

"I didn't say you were. Obviously, you're committed to your job and your daughter. So what's the problem between you and your sports editor?"

Peyton stared across the empty space between them, then steered the conversation in a safer direction. "Did you write to Ben? After Billy died?"

Eve shook her head. "I didn't see the point. Not after Richie told me Ben had married another woman."

"When was that?"

"Sometime in the seventies."

"But that was ages ago. Maybe Ben's divorced, or maybe—"

"Doesn't matter. Even if I wanted to, I wouldn't know how to find Ben Morrick. Wouldn't know where to start looking, not after all these years." Eve glanced at her watch. The friendliness in her manner tightened into an abrupt formality as she stood and moved toward her potter's wheel. "Though this has been lovely, I'm afraid you'll have to excuse me now. I really need to get to work."

With one smooth motion, Eve swept Peyton's pitiful approximation of a bowl off the potter's wheel, then dumped the clay into a plastic bag. Clearly the interview was over.

Peyton stood, her mind reeling with confusion. What happened to the gracious Southern lady who had greeted her and complimented her on the sandwiches? She could almost believe that something in the conversation had flipped a switch inside Eve Miller, vaporizing the hospitable hostess and leaving a remote, charmless creature in her place.

But what, exactly, could have done it?

Ignoring the chatter of the writers around her, Peyton sat at her desk and stared at the clock. Christine wouldn't get off work for another hour, which meant Peyton had time to make a start on the anniversary feature she planned to write about Eve Miller. Friday's column could wait until Thursday, and she could write her Sunday column at almost any point during the weekend.

If only Nora hadn't mentioned the possibility of syndication. If only she hadn't made a big deal about the upcoming anniversary. Writing this piece would be difficult enough without those added pressures.

Peyton's interview with Eve Miller had been less than satisfactory. What did she gain from it besides a couple of anecdotes and Eve's assurance that the world was now a different place? She could always discuss Eve's regret about not following her heart, of course, and mention that her marriage had been less than fulfilling. But those details did not exactly make a solid case for Eve's side in the passion versus caution debate.

At least Eve had given her another story thread to follow. Upon her return to the office, Peyton had asked Mandi to call the Navy and see if anyone in the veterans' department could trace Ben Morrick. Finding him would probably be as hard as roping the wind, but an interview with Ben would certainly add another dimension to the story.

Peyton turned toward her computer and gloomily considered the screen. How to begin? She hadn't written a feature in months, and coming up with a good lead was always a challenge.

She could begin with a quotation . . . if she could pin down a particular theme. She could begin with an anecdote, but which one? Maybe she could turn her crumpled attempt at pottery into a metaphor, comparing her disastrous efforts . . . to what, her first marriage? Eve's marriage to Billy?

She needed to focus. She'd told Nora that this would be a piece on passion versus reason, and that it would use Eve's belligerent letter as a hook. Okay, she had a starting point, but what to do with it?

She placed her fingers on the keyboard and bit her lower lip. Maybe she had a built-in advantage—why couldn't she create a feature that read like an extended Heart Healer column? Her readers were already used to her personal style. As long as she expanded this would-be column to feature length, Nora shouldn't object to the idea.

She drew a deep breath and began to type:

MacGruder, Peyton—Feature for Lifestyles section

Dear Reader:

As you might imagine, columnists receive all sorts of correspondence from readers. Many people write to thank us for a piece that struck them as particularly poignant; others fire off letters to add information to a topic we were required to cover in 750 words or less.

And then there are the other letters—the people who write to argue. Though I rarely meet those correspondents in person, in my mind's eye I often see them as red-faced, bellicose, and sweaty. Okay, so maybe that's not a fair perception, but since they choose not to launch their tirade at me face-to-face, I reserve the right to imagine them as I please.

I recently received an opposing viewpoint letter from a reader, yet I found it difficult to visualize this writer as anything less than dignified and gracious. Her point was well articulated, her prose sharp and properly punctuated. Rather than venting and withdrawing, the writer included an invitation to meet to discuss the matter further.

Intrigued, I accepted that invitation.

I found my correspondent to be everything I thought she'd be—articulate, lovely, gracious, and warm. Our initial conversation bloomed into a friendship, and her story has given me much to consider. Furthermore, her note happened to come at a time when I stood at a crossroads, and I'm beginning to wonder if Providence didn't orchestrate the entire experience so I could learn a valuable lesson.

But what lesson? I'm still struggling to put the pieces together.

Writing this article won't be easy—I've already made more false starts than I care to remember. But I hope you'll bear with me as I attempt to recount my experience of meeting with a woman who has forced me to take a hard look at the way I approach life: should our decisions be ruled by the head or by the heart? by caution or by passion?

My new friend once voted for caution; now she supports passion. I'm not certain she's right. Who wants to live in a world in which passion consistently rules restraint? On the *other hand, what drives great projects and impossible ventures? Passion.*

When we have to make a decision, which should we turn to?

Life is a series of forward motions, and I'll admit that I've been standing at an intersection of people and priorities for far too long. Yet how do we make forward progress when the past weighs on us like Marley's chains? With what tool can we cut those onerous bonds? Therapy? Confession?

Perhaps the answer can be found in a candid dialogue between friends. I've found a friend in this woman I'll identify only as "Eve." She lives in a stately brick home in an older part of town. If you met Eve on the street, you'd notice her quick smile and honest blue eyes—

Peyton looked up as Mandi stepped into her cubicle, a slip of paper in her hand and a victorious smile on her face. "Okay—" she waved the paper before Peyton's eyes—"I talked to a yeoman first class, whatever that is, at the veterans' administration. Very sexy voice, by the way. I'm betting he has a ship tattoo on—"

"Mandi." Peyton held out her hand. "Did you have information for me?"

"Right. Sorry." She placed the paper on Peyton's palm. "Bottom line, the last time the Navy had any contact with Ben Morrick was 1974. They sent his discharge papers to an address in Chiang Mai."

"Thailand?"

"Right."

Peyton studied the address. "Okay. It's a long shot, but here goes." She pulled a list from beneath a pile of books on her desk. "I've been gathering some research, too. These are the names of nongovernmental organizations operating in Asia. I'd like you to start calling and see if any of them have ever heard of Ben Morrick."

Mandi's eyes appeared to be in danger of falling out of her head. "Are you kidding? I'm pretty sure there are fewer names in the Beijing telephone directory."

Peyton glanced at her watch, then pushed away from her desk. "Maybe you'll get lucky and the first one will be the winner. If not, I'll give you a hand when I get back."

"You heading out?"

"For a while. Christine left me a message and asked me to stop by when she got home from work. I don't know what she couldn't discuss over the phone, but I'd better go see what she needs." Peyton shrugged her way into her jacket. "Hold the fort, will you? I'll be back soon."

Before stepping out of the car, Peyton checked the time on her cell phone. Two thirty, which meant Christine should have been home for at least fifteen minutes. Time enough to kick off her shoes and relax. Time enough for her to gather her thoughts about whatever she wanted to talk about.

Peyton locked her car and strode up the concrete sidewalk. No recycle bins on the curb today, no beer bottles outside the door. Maybe she shouldn't be noticing such things, but weren't mothers *supposed* to notice?

In any case, she felt relieved and grateful that Christine had called. Perhaps this meant she was beginning to think of Peyton naturally, as any girl would think of her mother when something urgent came up.

She rang the doorbell and waited until she heard the thump of steps in the foyer. A moment later Christine opened the door. Her face lit up like Times Square at dusk. "Hey! Thanks for coming by."

Peyton gave her a quick hug. "Everything all right? You sounded a little upset on the phone."

"I'm fine, but come on in. I do have something to tell you."

The words were enough to give any mother the willies, but Christine's eyes were clear and untroubled, so perhaps the calamity wasn't too awful. Peyton stepped into the foyer and noticed several boxes and trash bags against the wall. "You've been cleaning?"

"Yeah, this is stuff for the homeless shelter."

"Your dad's stuff?"

"And some of Mom's too. I kept the things that actually meant something, but the rest of it . . ." She shrugged. "I decided it's time to get my head straight—about a lot of things. Maybe start crossing that bridge you mentioned."

Peyton squeezed her daughter's shoulder. "I can't tell you how happy that makes me."

"Yeah. But hey, that's not why I called you."

"No?" Peyton gave her daughter another head-to-toe glance, her pulse quickening. "Are you sure you're okay?"

Christine laughed. "I'm fine. But I called you because Mike's bass player, Ricky, let it slip that David Danville's been crashing on his futon. Said he was supposed to keep it quiet because David's trying to avoid his dad."

Peyton gasped. "Who's been worried sick!"

"Yeah." Christine's brow furrowed as she bit her lip. "That's what I figured."

Peyton shook her head, astounded by the tendency of children, no matter what their age, to drive their parents crazy with worry. "Thanks for letting me know." She slipped her hands into her coat pockets. Now that she knew where David was—what should she do with the information?

"Here's the address." Christine pulled a card from a nearby table. "I asked you to stop by instead of calling because this house is right around the corner. I thought you might want to see him, but if you go over there, don't tell David I'm the one who dimed him out, okay?"

Peyton fingered the card thoughtfully. *If* she went over there . . . Should she? Was she still part of King's life, and should she remain involved in the problem with his son?

She pocketed the card and smiled. "Don't worry, sweetie. I never reveal a source."

"By the way," Christine asked, a guarded look shadowing her face, "how is the King these days?"

Peyton shook her head and shrugged. "Fine, I guess. He's been offered a job at the *New York Times*."

Christine's mouth dropped open. "He's not taking it, is he?"

"He might. After all, it's the *Times*."

"But—he—you—"

Peyton gave her a bitter smile. "I didn't accept his proposal, Chris. It just . . . I don't know, it didn't feel right."

Christine's brow lifted as uncertainty crept into her expression. "Didn't . . . *feel* . . . right?"

"Nothing for you to worry about." She pressed her hand to the curve of her daughter's cheek and then kissed the girl on the forehead. "I'll call you later."

On the way out to her car, Peyton stared at the address and considered her options. Should she drive back to the office and deliver this card to King? She hadn't seen him all day, but David was his son, not hers, and if she wasn't going to accept King's proposal, maybe she had no right to interfere in that relationship. On the other hand, even if her refusal to marry him resulted in the end of their relationship, she hoped King would always be a close friend. And David had confided in her, so she was already involved. What would it hurt if she drove over and talked to the boy for a few minutes? She might be able to help clear up the father-son miscommunication.

For King's sake, she would at least try to be a heart healer.

Peyton expected to pull up in front of a single-family residence, but the neglected two-story building before her looked more like a frat house. A columned porch jutted aggressively onto the lawn, and a weathered sign featuring a faded series of Greek letters had been nailed above the front door. Several of the windows stood open to the balmy spring breeze, and a trash can at the front door overflowed with pizza boxes and beer bottles. No flowers bloomed in the flower bed, and a well-worn path cut like a curving finger through the lawn and led to the porch.

Her mouth quirked. Maybe she should have worn a toga.

Someone had parked a motorcycle beneath the shade of an oak tree, and though Peyton usually couldn't tell one bike from another, she thought this one looked like David's. She crossed the lawn and climbed the steps to the front porch, then rang the bell. Nothing. She knocked on the screen door and waited, but no one answered.

So much for good intentions. She was halfway down the swollen wooden steps, resigned to surrendering the address to King, when she heard the squeak of the front door. She turned and saw David standing on the porch, dressed in jeans and a wrinkled T-shirt. He thrust one hand in his pocket and peered at her through bleary eyes. "Peyton?"

She forced a smile. "Hey there."

"What are you doing here?" He jerked his thumb at the sprained screen door. "You know someone who lives here?"

"I know you. I came to tell you to phone home, E.T., before your parents have to be institutionalized. They're both worried sick about you."

He blew out a breath. "Message received. Anything else? 'Cause I have to get to work."

Peyton straightened her spine. "Just one other thing: I didn't say anything. Your *coach* told your dad. That's how he found out about your being cut from the baseball team. I wouldn't betray your trust."

He scratched at his neck as one corner of his mouth rose in a smirk. "Makes sense, I guess. Sorry. For the way I acted the other day, I mean. I was a little wound up."

"We all get wound up sometimes." She took a step closer to him. "I'm not going to make a speech or anything, so don't start rolling your eyes. But I do want to say one thing."

He leaned against the doorframe as if bracing himself for a lashing. "Fire away."

"It's just this." Peyton swallowed hard. "I don't expect you to know this, but my father and I spent our lives talking *at* one another, not *to* one another. Most of the time we didn't talk at all, but it wasn't his fault. Nearly every time he reached out to me, I turned away. And now that he's gone, I can't tell you how much I regret my actions."

David lifted a brow in what looked like amused contempt. "Maybe you should tell my dad the same story."

"Maybe I should." She crossed her arms and exhaled a sharp breath. "But your father and I are sort of taking a breather."

He gave her a blank look, his surprise evidenced only by a wary twitch of one eye. "Yeah? That's funny. That's what my dad said the day before my mom filed for divorce."

Peyton flinched, the words striking like a pang in her heart. As much as she'd tried to brace herself for all possibilities, David's words had just reminded her that dissolution was not only *possible* but *probable*.

A sudden flare of fury almost choked her. She marched back up the steps, extending one finger like a scolding schoolteacher. "Don't be so snide, David! Sarcasm is ugly and hurtful. And as for your dad and me . . ." She halted as words failed her. What should she say? What *could* she say?

She hesitated, then waved her hand and turned away. "Never mind about us," she called over her shoulder. "You and your dad need to get things straightened out. I need to get back to the office."

She was almost at her car when David called her name. "I'm sorry," he yelled, loud enough to wake anyone who might be napping upstairs. "I didn't mean it."

She drew a deep breath, then turned. "Really."

"Wait." He jogged down the steps and hurried toward her, then braced one arm on the front of the car and tried on a smile that seemed a size too small. "I've got this job, see, at a one-hour photo place. The one at the corner of Main and Walnut."

With her keys in hand, Peyton lifted a brow, waiting.

"If you see my dad, tell him I'm working four to eleven every night. You know, in case he wants to drop by."

She searched his face and felt her heart soften when she saw concern crinkling the corners of his eyes. This young man was so much like King—gruff and tough on the outside but tender where it mattered.

A knot rose in her throat. "I'll tell him," she promised.

Fifteen

ARMED WITH A good excuse to look for King, Peyton stepped off the elevator and turned right, moving down the aisle that led to the editors' offices. Activity in the writers' cubicles had mostly ceased for the day, as many of the reporters had filed their stories and gone home. By four o'clock the editors were usually scrambling in their offices, rushing to edit copy, place features, and reserve space for any late-breaking reports—

But quiet emanated from King's office. She hesitated outside his open door and gazed at his empty desk. His computer screen saver, a tribute to the old Pong game, blipped at her without offering any clues as to where he might be.

She wracked her brain, trying to remember if King had mentioned an interview or another out-of-town trip. Because he'd spent all day yesterday in New York, he should have been stuck in the office today, playing catch-up. Then again, he might be anywhere in Middleborough, on a frantic search for David.

She shook her head. She'd call King's cell phone, give him her news, and tell him not to worry. David was safe; he was even willing to talk. A calm conversation between those two would be a huge step forward.

She turned a corner and nearly ran into Mandi.

"Oh!" The girl tapped her chest with a fluttering hand. "Thank goodness. I was hoping to find you before I went home."

Peyton smiled. "I told you I'd be back. Any luck with the NGOs?"

Mandi kept pace with Peyton as they navigated the cubicle maze that led to her desk. "That's what I wanted to tell you. I had to call about fifty places, but I finally struck gold."

Peyton's mind went blank with shock. "You found Ben Morrick?"

The intern broke into a wide grin. "It wasn't easy. Seems like I talked to every dot-org in Asia to do it, but yeah, I found him. By the way, you might want to give Nora a heads-up about the gigandus phone bill coming her way."

Peyton dropped into her chair and gaped at the girl. "So . . . give me details."

Mandi leaned on Peyton's desk, her face rapt. "Like I said, on about the fiftieth call, I found an NGO Ben had flown with for nearly ten years. Apparently their job was to shuttle orphans, sick people, and medical supplies in and out of remote mission outposts, that sort of thing."

"Is Ben still in the jungle?"

"You consider Washington, D.C., a jungle? Because a lot of people do."

Peyton took a wincing breath. "Ben Morrick is as close as D.C.?"

"Lives just inside the Beltway. Retired to an address in Virginia about six months ago."

Peyton leaned back in her chair, thrilled by this small but satisfying bit of news. "You got all this from one phone call?"

"The guy I spoke to at the nonprofit's home office in Hong Kong was very friendly. Invited me for dim sum."

"That's great, Mandi." Peyton's smile broadened in approval. "Your new friend offer up an address?"

With a flourish, Mandi produced a printed page from her pocket. "Indeed he did. You're going to have to take your act on the road, though, if you want to talk to him. Ben Morrick's got no e-mail and his phone's unlisted. The guy must be old-school."

"I don't mind a road trip." Peyton took the paper from Mandi and studied the address, then beamed at the girl. "I don't know how much they're paying interns these days, but you, young lady, deserve a raise!"

"Wow." Mandi fanned her face as if embarrassed. "Feel free to mention that to Nora, if you want. Or just tell her to hire me when the semester's over."

"I will," Peyton promised, turning to her computer. "You're going to make a fine reporter."

After printing out driving directions from her home to Ben Morrick's address in Alexandria, Virginia, Peyton spent several minutes looking up Internet references to Wings of Mercy, the private philanthropic organization that had hired Ben Morrick to transport orphans after the war. The Wings of Mercy home page featured several black-and-white photographs that tore at her heart. Eve had not spent a lot of time describing Ben Morrick's personality, but he must be man of rare kindness if he had remained in Asia to help boys and girls like these.

Or did he remain in Asia because he knew his first love had married someone else?

Shaking her head, Peyton clicked to another page of photographs and stared into the almond-shaped eyes of pitifully thin orphans. Her heart twisted. If war had visited American shores and torn Christine from the only parents she had ever known, what would have happened to her? She might look like these little girls, thin and starved for nourishment and affection.

But Christine had been adored and cherished by parents who were able to give her what Peyton could not.

Staring at the photographs, Peyton had to admit that she'd been harboring a quiet jealousy of Christine's adoptive parents. She loved the girl every bit as much as they did, yet to them went the privilege of raising her, hearing her laughter, receiving her childhood hugs and kisses. And though the three of them must have endured *some* hard times, Christine had been a healthy child and a good kid. Raising her couldn't have been terribly traumatic.

She sighed. Then again, maybe Christine's goodness was the result of her adoptive parents' wholesome values. Nurture and nature—both were required to raise a healthy child. She'd provided the genetic gifts, but that dear couple had done the nurturing.

And parenting certainly wasn't easy. She'd been an active parent for less than three months, long enough to gain a deep and unswerving respect for anyone who took on the task. King was always telling her not to sweat it, that she'd learn by doing, but he wasn't around to encourage her today—

Where *was* the man?

She stood and surveyed the sea of the cubicles, then checked the door of his office—still open, with no signs of life within. On a whim, she swiveled and looked toward the stairwell. Whenever King wanted to work without distraction or interruption, he used to grab his laptop and escape the office hubbub.

Following her hunch, she left her desk and headed toward the stairs, ignoring the end-of-day banter between two coworkers. She pressed on the old oak exit door and stepped onto the landing, then glanced up the stairs.

"What a surprise." King's fingers froze on his keyboard. "Usually only fitness freaks and fire marshals take the stairs."

Overcome with relief, she smiled and closed the door behind her. "Stopped by your office. Thought maybe you'd given up on us yokels and gone back to New York."

He shook his head. "Just wanted to get some work done. I'm seriously behind."

She hesitated, aware of the tension stretching between them. Could they still be friends . . . or had she hurt him too badly?

"I was going to call you," she began.

His expression turned hopeful. "Really?"

"About David."

He blinked. "What about David?"

Peyton moved to the banister and leaned on the newel. "Christine found out that he's staying at a frat house not far from her place. I just came from there."

Concern and confusion flickered in his eyes. "Is he okay?"

"He's fine."

King's shoulders slumped in relief. "I've got to call his mother and let her know." All business now, he closed his laptop and stood.

"He's crashing with a friend from school," Peyton hurried to add. "And he's working. Evenings, from four till eleven. At a photo shop on the corner of Main and Walnut."

King nodded as he moved down the stairs. "I know the one."

"He said you can stop by if you want. To talk."

After reaching the landing, King paused by the door. "I think I will. Thanks." Something stirred in his eyes as he looked at her. "Anything else?"

Yes—I miss you.

But she couldn't voice that thought. She had surrendered her claim on him, so now it was only fair that he define what remained of their relationship.

A lump rose in her throat, threatening to choke off her voice. But she needed to speak of other things, safer things, so somehow she pushed the words out. "I was reminded of something recently."

With one hand on the doorknob, he gave her a distracted nod. "What's that?"

"Someone told me that no one achieves success without first

finding the courage to face potential failure. David has that kind of courage, you know. He just needs to know that whether he succeeds or fails at this attempt at a career in art, you'll always be there for him."

A flash that could have been skepticism shone in King's eyes, and for a moment she thought he was going to say something glib about taking parenting advice from a neophyte. But he only nodded and turned toward the exit.

She looked wistfully at his hand on the doorknob. "I guess that's all I wanted to say."

"Well, it's not all I have to say." King released the door and turned to face her, wrapping his arms around his laptop. When he met her gaze, the usual expression of easygoing contentment had gone missing from the depths of his eyes. "I'm glad we have this chance to talk because I'd like to get something off my chest."

"Okay." Peyton tightened her grip on the newel post. "Fire away."

King swallowed. "I know you feel you owe Christine your full attention, and that's fine; I understand why you might not want to get married right now. But don't confuse maternal obligation with penance for having given her up in the first place. Don't deny yourself the life you deserve. Because in the long run, you're going to hurt yourself and your daughter. You're going to be lonely, MacGruder, and take it from me—alone and guilt-ridden is not a good place to be."

She arched a brow, wondering if she should make an offhand comment about taking relationship advice from a man who barely spoke to his ex-wife; then she noticed the look of agonized frustration in his eyes.

She had done this. She had kept him at arm's length, stalled him, and finally pushed him away. She had hurt him, and she had no one to blame but herself.

"Thanks," she said, her voice breaking. "I'll keep that in mind."

They stared at each other for a long moment before she looked away, freeing him to turn, open the door, and leave her in the stairwell with nothing but the echoes of their voices.

"Alone and guilt-ridden is not a good place to be."

Like some kind of dire prophecy, King's words kept replaying in Peyton's mind as she drove out of the *Times* parking lot. She tried to mute his voice by forcing a smile and telling herself that life would go on. She turned on the radio and punched several preset buttons, searching for music that didn't sound like a dirge for lost love and the end of the world.

"Life will go on." Peyton repeated the phrase again as she turned onto Eve Miller's street. No matter what happened between her and King, life would continue more or less as usual. If he decided to stay in Middleborough, they would eventually be able to speak without stumbling over all the things they'd left unsaid. Maybe they'd even be able to laugh together again. He'd have no trouble finding another woman who appreciated his considerable charm and warmth, and maybe he'd be fortunate enough to find a companion who actually liked sports. He'd be better off, really, while Peyton would be—

"Fine." She spoke the word aloud as she turned the switch and killed the ignition. She glanced toward Eve's house and was pleased to see the bicycle leaning against the garden fence.

So what if Peyton didn't have a grand love in her life? She'd been married, so it wasn't like she was missing out on the experience. She was now at a different place; now she could concentrate on her daughter. She intended to relish every moment she and Christine spent together because they had years of catching up to do.

Come to think of it, so did Eve Miller.

Peyton slid out of the car and crossed the street, then stepped through the wrought iron gate and hurried toward the front door. The day was nearly spent and she didn't want to interrupt Eve's dinner, but this news couldn't wait—and it needed to be delivered in person. Though Eve had been rather brusque when they last parted, Peyton's announcement might change her attitude.

Before she could climb the front porch steps, the door opened and Eve stepped out. She navigated her way down the porch stairs, then looked up and gasped. "Peyton! I didn't expect to see you there."

Peyton stepped forward. "I'm sorry I didn't call, but I thought I might drop by to deliver some news. But if you're in a hurry, it can wait."

Eve shook her head and smiled, once again a picture of graciousness. "No hurry. I'm just off to the gallery for a bit."

"Then I won't keep you, but I had to share our news."

Eve gazed at her with a bland half smile. "Good news about you and the sports editor?"

"Not exactly. It's your news, Eve. We found Ben Morrick."

Eve's expression didn't change for a moment; then the words fell into place with an almost-audible click. Shock flickered over her face like heat lightning.

Peyton smiled, pleased with the effects of her announcement. "I knew you'd be surprised. But here's the best part—Ben lives less than two hundred miles away. He's in Alexandria, Virginia, just outside of D.C."

Eve gave Peyton a sidelong glance of utter disbelief; then she pushed past Peyton and strode through her garden gate. Moving almost robotically, she pulled her bike off the fence and mounted the seat.

Peyton followed, a note card in her hand. "I have his address, if you—"

"I'm sorry," Eve interrupted, her tone shifting to frosty politeness, "but I really have to go."

"Eve—" Peyton caught hold of the handlebars. "Wait a moment, please. From what you've told me about Ben, I'm sure he'd love to see you again."

"Ms. MacGruder." Eve's voice was like chilled steel. "Would you please release my bicycle?"

Peyton lifted her hands in a don't-shoot pose and backed away, stunned into silence as Eve pedaled onto the street and vanished into the gathering dusk.

Sixteen

THE BRISK AUTUMN wind blew through Eve's hair as she stood on her bike and pedaled with all the energy she could muster. A car honked as she zipped through an intersection without slowing, but the sound barely registered in her consciousness. What did it matter if she was struck and killed? If she didn't reach Ben in time, her life might as well be over anyway.

She sat back on the narrow seat and gripped the handlebars, skimming over the gutter and following the signs to Sewell's Point. A moment later the Newport News Naval Air Station came into view, a blur of white buildings fronted by retired jets and set against a backdrop of hulking gray ships.

When a ribbon of sweat trickled down her spine, she knew her blouse would soon be sticking to her ribs. This wasn't the way she had planned to tell Ben she loved him; this wasn't the romantic farewell she had imagined. But once she'd found the courage to tell him she was willing to defy her family, urgency demanded that she move quickly. She had to see Ben at once, and her landlady would have had too many questions if she'd asked to borrow the car.

Eve lowered her head when she spied the checkpoint at the side of the road. A uniformed soldier stood at the guard shack, as always. He held a clipboard as he bent forward and spoke to the driver of a shiny new sedan. If she were quick and quiet, she might be able to squeeze through the narrow opening between the barrier and the guard shack; if she entered through the exit, the guard might not even notice her arrival.

But the thought of Ben's imminent departure rose again in her mind, sending a flash of grief through her. Nausea followed that sinking feeling, stealing her energy and turning her knees to mush. The shiny sedan pulled ahead as the striped barrier rose, and perspiration dampened her hairline as she struggled to push the bike toward the checkpoint.

She bent over the handlebars when she saw the guard look down to write on his clipboard. The sedan crawled forward, the striped barrier waited at attention, and Eve ducked lower on her bike and begged her legs to keep pumping. The brisk wind, which had blown directly into her face since leaving home, suddenly decided to cooperate and propelled her toward the naval base and the man she had come to see.

The guard looked up and saw her. His jaw dropped when she veered toward the left, and he realized she had no intention of stopping. "Hey," he shouted, one hand rising. "You can't do that. Stop! You hear me? Stop!"

Eve ducked lower and kept pedaling, holding her breath as her bike passed between the security post and the striped barrier at the exit. Now she would *really* have to hurry, because the guard was undoubtedly calling the military police to report that an unidentified young woman had just entered the base without clearance or permission.

Fortunately, he had no idea where she was going.

She passed the startled driver of the sedan and pointed her bike toward the barracks. Once she'd turned the corner, she straightened her spine and forced herself to breathe deeply and regularly as she searched for the officers' quarters. If she had to stop and ask for directions, she couldn't look like a panicked fugitive from justice.

There! After spotting the marker she was seeking, she aimed the bike toward a green hill, rode over the grass until gravity slowed her; then she leaped off the seat and let the bicycle fall to the grass. Arms pumping, she ran up the short steps and flew through the doorway, then forced herself to walk down the glistening hallway at a steady, more dignified pace.

First floor, he'd said. His room was the first door on the right.

But the first door on the right stood open, and the two beds inside had been stripped to the mattresses. The lockers gaped; the small bedside table was bare. Impossible, because Ben had told her that he kept that picture of the four of them beside his bed. So she must be in the wrong building or on the wrong floor. . . .

But she wasn't.

Cold reality swept over her in a punishing wave, nearly knocking her off her feet. She stepped back into the hallway, struggling for breath, as a gurgling sound rose around the lump in her throat. This was his room and no mistake. But Ben Morrick no longer lived here.

She was too late.

"Hold it right there, missy."

Eve turned and blinked away a rush of tears. A pair of MPs were striding down the hallway, their walk stiff with purpose. Neither wore a smile.

She waited until they reached her before speaking. "I know I'm in trouble—" her words tumbled over each other in her hurry to learn the hard truth—"but just tell me, please. How long ago?"

The older man glanced past her and saw the empty room. His eyes softened. "Batch of them shipped out this morning. They're over the Pacific by now."

The younger MP began to say something, but the senior partner held up a silencing hand. He took Eve's arm, but his grip was gentle. "Boyfriend?"

She felt her mouth quirk in a sad attempt at a smile. "More than that."

"Didn't he tell you when he was shipping out?"

She shook her head. "I had no idea it would be this soon. I . . . I don't think he wanted me counting the days."

The guard settled his free hand on his belt. "I'm sorry. Afraid you're going to have to come with us, though, Miss . . ."

Eve blinked, barely hearing the words. "Miss? Oh. Jackson. Eve Jackson."

"This way, Miss Jackson."

The guard turned her toward the hallway, and Eve could barely summon the energy to keep up with her escort.

She who hesitates is lost. The words of the old proverb seeped through her sorrow, enfolding her in a cocoon of anguish.

Seventeen

AFTER DINNER, PEYTON held the phone against her ear and paced in the kitchen. "If you're home, please pick up."

Eve had said she was off to the gallery "for a bit," which meant she was probably back home by now . . . and screening her calls.

Peyton waited for a long moment, then decided to keep talking. "What happened to our deal? the two-way street? the give-and-take? We were both supposed to get something out of our conversation, remember? I told you an entire story, but all I've gotten from you is a teaser, a couple of anecdotes, and about a dozen more questions. My feature is due on Thursday and I'm not happy with what I've written so far. It feels . . . disjointed. So call me, please. You have the number."

She hung up and dropped the phone back into its charger. She looked at her kitchen island and the single place mat on the bar, then shifted her gaze to the empty chair where King usually sat.

King wouldn't be coming over tonight. Christine would be a

no-show, too. Of course, Peyton didn't expect to see her daughter every day; the girl was eighteen and on the verge of independence. Soon she'd return to college, and when the semester began, she'd be busy almost all the time with studies, friends, activities, and her job . . .

While Peyton stayed home and ate frozen dinners on her single place mat.

"Alone and guilt-ridden is not a good place to be."

Blocking the intrusive voice from her mind, she drew a heavy breath and moved to the foyer table, where she'd dropped her briefcase. After pulling out several pages, she found the map with directions to Ben Morrick's address.

Two hundred miles translated to four hours, give or take a little traffic. She had no deadline tomorrow, so she could afford to spend eight hours on the road. Nora wouldn't be looking for her, and neither would King.

And she had to finish this feature. If Eve wouldn't explain why she had suddenly clammed up, Peyton would interview another witness to the events in question.

She would drive to Alexandria and meet Ben Morrick.

Eighteen

SHORTLY AFTER NOON on Wednesday, Peyton slowed outside Ben Morrick's country cottage. She parked across the street and took a few minutes to study the house. An explosion of vibrant bulbs bloomed in the beds along the walkway, a wealth of tulips, daffodils, and hyacinths, the first arrivals of spring.

She turned in her seat and searched the property for signs of a wife's presence: two cars, a frilly nightgown on a clothesline, or a pair of pink slippers by the front door. She saw nothing that attested to the presence of a woman in the house, but she'd still be cautious. Mrs. Morrick might not appreciate a stranger dropping in with news of her husband's old girlfriend. On the other hand, a smiling photo of the Morricks might help assuage Eve's regrets.

Peyton dropped her digital camera into her purse and got out of the car. She walked toward the house and stopped when she spied a man on his knees beside the flower bed. She hadn't been able to see him from across the street.

The man set down a pair of clippers and wiped his hand on the Hawaiian shirt he wore. With a pair of pink tulips in his other hand, he squinted up at Peyton. "Can I help you?"

Her eyes flicked to the door, registered the house number, and returned to the gardener. "I'm looking for Ben Morrick."

"Is he in some kind of trouble?"

"No, not at all."

"Then you've found him."

She drew a deep breath. "Good. I'm Peyton MacGruder, a reporter for the *Middleborough Times*, and I've just driven two hundred miles to see you. I'm bringing news of an old friend."

His gaze drifted over his greening flower bed before he pushed himself up from the grass. "Might as well invite you in, then. Sounds like this conversation might go better with coffee."

Once inside the house, Peyton accepted a coffee mug and perched on a kitchen barstool. "Nice place you've got here, Mr. Morrick. Your flowers are beautiful."

"Thanks." He filled his mug with the fragrant brew. "You can call me Ben. My wife got me into gardening. Said it would be the yin to the yang of my flying choppers."

Peyton lifted her mug and smiled above the rim. "She sounds like a wise woman."

"She was indeed."

"Are you still . . . ?"

"She passed away three years ago. Ovarian cancer."

"I'm sorry."

Ben sat on a stool opposite her and picked up the business card she'd dropped on the counter. While he examined it, Peyton sipped her coffee and studied him.

The passing of forty years had thinned the man's hair somewhat, but the brown eyes hadn't changed from the photo in Eve's workroom. Laugh lines radiated from his eyes and the parentheses around his mouth didn't age him so much as give him a look of resolve. The strong jaw was still present, and at this distance, Peyton could see that Ben Morrick had a most attractive cleft in his chin.

She had a feeling more than a few movie stars had endured plastic surgery for clefts like that.

"So," Ben finally said, dropping her card, "tell me what brings you all the way up from North Carolina. And why should a reporter care anything about me and my old buddies?"

Peyton lowered her mug. "The other day I received a letter in the mail—a note from Eve Miller. I believe you knew her as Eve Jackson."

The name definitely registered with Ben. When he spoke again, his voice came out strangled. "Evie? You've heard from Evie?"

Peyton nodded. "She wrote to complain, actually. About a column I'd written."

Ben's eyes narrowed. "Doesn't sound like Evie. What sort of column did you write?"

Peyton laughed. "I didn't think I said anything to elicit that kind of reaction. Specifically, I was discussing when it's advisable to trust your head and when it's better to trust your emotions. I said that when it came to matters of the heart, caution should always trump passion. I received several reader letters about that column, most of them supportive . . . except for Eve's."

The man's feathery white brows shot up to his hairline. "Evie voted for charging ahead?"

"She did. And she said my opinion was idiotic."

A twisted smile crossed Ben Morrick's face; then he stood and moved to the window. "I'm still listening," he called without looking over his shoulder.

"Eve's letter led to several conversations at her home," Peyton went on. "When I visited, she told me about Richie, Billy, and . . . you."

He turned, one eyebrow arched. "I wish I could have been a fly on the wall. What'd she tell you?"

Peyton smiled. "She told me how you three men trained together. About the friendship you shared. And about how you once encouraged her to cross a gorge on the railing of a bridge."

He chuckled and lifted his mug. "*Gorge* is a bit of an overstatement."

"I don't think so. She implied that the action was a dangerous step for her, literally and figuratively."

Ben made his way back to the kitchen counter, a cloud settling on his face. Peyton hesitated, confused by his expression, then decided to proceed with caution. "She said the two of you became . . . *close* after that."

He dropped a sprinkling of sugar into his coffee, gave it a quick stir, and stared into his cup as if he were seeing reflections of the past in its liquid contents. "That was . . . a long time ago."

Peyton backpedaled a bit. "I assume you knew she and Billy got married, right?"

Ben nodded. "Richie Franks told me when we ran into each other in Saigon. He said Billy's father pulled a few strings and got him a stateside posting . . . as a wedding present."

"Were you surprised? By their marriage?"

He shifted his gaze to the kitchen window again. "Yes—and no. It's certainly what their parents wanted. To further their own agendas." He sighed. "Still, it was hard to believe Eve would settle; she was so curious, so alive. And Billy—he was just the opposite. She deserved better. She deserved . . ."

"What?"

The thin line of his lips clamped tight, and his Adam's apple bobbed as he swallowed. "More than Billy was capable of offering."

"But there was nothing you could do or say, right? Eve isn't exactly forthcoming when it comes to certain details, so I've been trying to read between the lines. I figure that Billy was your best friend and she'd already agreed to marry him, so you felt you couldn't declare what you must have been feeling."

Ben's jaw tightened as he stared out the window; wherever they'd been in 1966, he was on his way back.

"Quite a dilemma," Peyton finished.

Ben nodded absently. "You could say that."

"So . . . how did you resolve it?"

"In the worst way imaginable, I'm afraid." He turned and focused on Peyton. "What did Eve tell you about how it ended? Between us, I mean?"

"She was . . . vague. Which is why I'm here, I suppose. To get your side of things."

He propped one hand on the counter, affecting a nonchalant pose. "And why does it matter?"

"Because my readers will want to know."

"Why should your readers care a whit about a couple of people who *didn't* get married forty years ago?"

The question hovered between them, and Peyton thought hard as she formed a careful answer. "Because . . . my readers learn from the stories of others. And so do I."

He looked at her, thought working in his eyes.

"Eve led me to believe that she sincerely regrets not following her heart," Peyton added, eager to fill the silence. "As to why she didn't, I don't know; she won't say. So . . . will you tell me what happened between you two?"

The man stared into his coffee mug for a long minute; then he lifted his head. "A couple of weeks before I shipped out, a squall line blew in from the sea. I was driving through the rain when I saw Eve on the road ahead, riding that silly bicycle of hers. I probably should have kept going, but she was getting soaked and I wanted to protect her. . . ."

Nineteen

BEN LEANED FORWARD to peer through the bleary arcs created by his thumping windshield wipers. Yes, that was Eve up ahead; he'd recognize that blonde ponytail anywhere. He gunned the engine and passed her, then pulled over to the shoulder, shoved the gear into park, and ran out into the storm.

"Ben?" She stopped her bike and straddled it, blinking at him in the rain.

"Get in the car," he ordered, grabbing the handlebars. "You're going to catch pneumonia."

For a moment he thought she'd argue, but she stepped over the bike and sprinted toward the passenger door. He opened the trunk and heaved the bike inside, then hurried back to the driver's seat.

Eve was shivering in the car, her teeth rattling like castanets as he slipped the key into the ignition. "Here." He reached for his flight jacket in the backseat. "Put this around you and warm yourself up."

Again, she did as she was told without debate. He peered at her, wondering if she was coming down with something. A flush had brightened her damp cheeks, so maybe she was running a fever. "Honestly, Evie, I can't believe you'd go out in this rain. A car could hit you or run you off the road; I nearly didn't see you myself."

She glared at him, her lower jaw trembling as her teeth chattered. "The rain . . . c-c-c-came up . . . s-s-s-suddenly."

He tore his gaze away from her and cranked the engine. "Let me get the heat on. Don't worry; I'll have you safe and warm in just a minute."

For once the car responded immediately, the engine purring as the heater poured a stream of warm air into the car. Ben shifted gears and drove slowly, looking for the narrow side street that would lead him back to Evie's apartment.

"So." He cleared his throat, uncomfortably aware that her wet dress looked as unsubstantial as paper over her trembling legs. "Were you on your way home?"

Still trembling, she shook her head. "I was just out for a ride."

"Going where?"

"Anywhere. I w-w-wanted to get away. I needed some t-t-time alone . . . to think about things."

He cast her a curious glance. "What kind of things?"

She didn't answer, but her eyes went as big and round as full moons. A curious stirring troubled his belly as the back of his mouth went dry.

"You getting warmer?" he asked, aware that she was sitting closer to him than to the door. Not exactly girlfriend close, but close enough.

She nodded. "Your jacket . . . feels very nice."

He turned, determined to keep his eyes on the road. "If you're looking for something to do . . . you want to go play pool?"

She took a deep breath, then exhaled it abruptly. "No."

"Want to go downtown?"

"Looking like a drowned rat?" She laughed. "No."

"Okay, then. What do you want to do?"

Her fine, silky brows rose a trifle. "Who says we have to do anything? You don't have to entertain me, Ben. I enjoy just being with you."

He smiled as a warm glow flowed through him. For this afternoon, at least, he wouldn't have to compete with Billy. He could look at Eve without tempering his expression; he could enjoy her company without feeling Billy's shadow across his heart.

"So . . . you just want to find a pretty spot and talk? Maybe I can help you sort through some of those things you were thinking about."

"Maybe you can . . . if I don't freeze first."

"Poor baby." He took his right hand off the wheel and slipped his arm around her shoulders, then reached beneath his jacket to warm her bare arm. Her skin felt like satin beneath his palm, soft and pliable and cool.

He tensed when she turned to him, expecting a rebuke. But her blue eyes were wide and approving as she whispered, "Thanks. That feels wonderful."

Emboldened, he turned the car down a dirt road that led to a falling-down shack no one had lived in for years. At the end of the drive, he parked beneath a tall yellow hickory. When the engine had stilled, he leaned against his door, pulling Eve close to warm her against his chest. Despite the awkwardness of maneuvering around the steering wheel, she snuggled into him, fitting beneath his arm like she'd been made for that spot. He tugged his jacket over her like a blanket, and for a long time they sat without speaking, the silence broken only by falling hickory nuts and the slowing patter of raindrops.

From the moment Ben took her into his arms, he battled the urge to kiss her. Billy Miller didn't deserve this girl; Billy didn't appreciate the woman behind the pretty face. But Ben had glimpsed her artistic talents; he had laughed at her jokes; he had faith in her abilities to charge into the world and make it a better place.

If she married Billy, she'd probably end up sitting in a fine house, surrounded by knickknacks and silver tea trays. Ben would do anything to stand between Evie and that stuffy fate, but she had made her choice. Her parents and Billy's were certainly pushing her, but no one was holding a gun to her head; no one was forcing her to wear Billy's ring.

But her parents were a formidable force, and for months Ben had struggled against the knowledge that he was fighting a losing battle. Still, for this hour at least, Eve was here, Eve was his. For this afternoon, they were free to acknowledge the feelings that had bloomed between them.

When the rain stopped, she'd sit up and announce that she needed to be getting back. He'd drive her home, and maybe she'd give him a chaste peck on the cheek as a thank-you for pulling her out of the rain. Maybe.

He had resigned himself to that scenario when Eve turned her head to look into his face. "Comfortable?" he murmured, looking down at her.

He felt a jolt when he saw that her blue eyes brimmed with threatening tears. "How," she whispered, her voice ragged, her fingertips rising to caress his chin, "can I let you go all the way to Vietnam?"

She meant *him*, not Billy or Richie. And those tears! Those glittering diamonds were his undoing. He stroked her cheek and they splashed over her face, burning his fingertips, scalding his palms, searing his lips . . .

Her tears broke through every wall he'd managed to erect against her.

Twenty

"AFTERWARD," BEN SAID, his face a study in defeat, "I begged her to let me confront Billy, to lay our secret out on the table, but she kept shaking her head and saying that the situation was impossible because two families were counting on this marriage. I was sure we could work things out—eventually we could be forgiven our transgression and released from our previous obligations. I even offered to marry her right away, before I had to ship out."

Peyton nodded, imagining the stubborn set of Eve's face. Even at that young age, she would have been a formidable opponent. "But Eve wouldn't—"

"She wouldn't hear of it. You have to understand—things were different back then, especially in society. The invitations had been engraved, the parties all set. Eve climbed out of the car, gave me one last kiss, and yanked her bike out of the trunk. I tried to stop her, but she—well, she was a determined woman. Strong, opinionated . . . and beautiful."

Peyton felt a smile rise at the corner of her mouth. "She hasn't changed much. After that day, did you ever see her again?"

"I wanted to, desperately, but the choice wasn't mine to make. It was hers . . . and she stayed away. I shipped out, she got married, and I went off to fly choppers. After the war, I met a woman who helped heal my ragged edges, so I married her. We had a good life together until she died." His eyes warmed slightly as he lifted his coffee mug. "And that's the story of my life, Ms. MacGruder. Are you sorry you asked?"

Peyton studied Ben Morrick, then reached into her bag and removed a pen and notepad. She scribbled an address on a blank page and tore it out. "You knew Billy was killed, right? A sailing accident. *Years* ago."

Ben sipped from his cup, then looked away. "I didn't know."

She slid the address across the counter. "This is Eve Miller's phone number. She lives only four hours away."

Ben took the paper, his hand trembling slightly, stared at it, and handed it back to Peyton. "I'm afraid, Ms. MacGruder, that it's still Eve's choice to make."

"But—"

"Call me old-fashioned." He smiled and rested his chin on his hand. "But I still believe a gentleman does not force his attention upon a lady."

King waited while a mother herded two children through the intersection before he pulled into the public parking lot nearest the one-hour photo shop on Main Street. Downtown was nearly deserted at this hour; the only businesses still open were the photo place and an all-night drugstore in the next block. A light rain had fallen shortly after sunset, so the roads were glossy and wet, reflecting the streetlights and the neon welcome sign in the one-hour photo.

He locked his car and slid his hands into his pockets, surveying the nearly empty area. David's motorcycle stood parked at the curb, so Peyton's information had been correct. He was inside, working and waiting . . . for what, another confrontation?

His stomach knotted at the thought of Peyton. She had made herself scarce at the office today, not even stopping by to check her mail, and he hadn't had the courage to ask Mandi if Peyton had called in sick or to say she was working from home. Yesterday she had behaved almost normally, talking to him as if they were coworkers and good friends, but he couldn't be around her long and pretend he was content to be a sometime *boyfriend*. He loved the woman, loved her in a commit-for-life sort of way, and if she couldn't love him back . . .

Was he crazy for loving that woman?

New York was looking better and better. But that would mean leaving not only the woman and the paper he loved, but David, too. Although David might be leaving soon, himself. Sounded like the kid was bent on wearing a beret and drawing caricatures on the streets of Los Angeles or some other urban center.

A bell jangled above the photo shop door as he entered. A kid in a Panthers T-shirt glanced up from a handheld video game, then reluctantly shifted his attention to King. "Hey, can I help you?"

"Maybe." King glanced around but saw no sign of David in the store or behind the counter. "I'm looking for my son. I was told that he works here—"

"Your son named David?"

"Yes."

"He's in the darkroom." The kid pointed to a swinging door behind the cash register. "You can go on back, but don't go in the darkroom if the warning light's on, okay?"

"Got it."

King pushed his way through a small gate and walked through the open doorway. He found himself in a workroom where a giant processing machine hummed and clicked while it spit out color prints. Another door led to an adjacent room with a rectangular warning light above the door. The light wasn't lit.

He approached the door cautiously, afraid of ruining someone's photographs as well as his relationship with David. The door was cracked, and through the narrow opening, he could see his son working, intent on a series of long rectangular trays as he transferred large prints from one chemical bath to another.

Knowing that timing could be crucial in photo development, King leaned against the doorframe and waited until David had finished. "That looks complicated."

David turned, his dark eyes widening. "Oh—hi." He dried his hands on a towel and leaned against the table. After a moment of awkward silence, he managed a crooked smile. "Didn't think you'd actually come by."

King tried not to show that the remark stung. "Why wouldn't I? You're my son and I've been worried about you."

"I've been your son all my life, but sometimes you weren't exactly close by, you know?"

King cleared his throat. "Okay. Guilty as charged. But during those times, I wasn't around for reasons that had nothing to do with you."

David crossed his arms, his lips thinning. "I get that, I guess. Divorce can be hard on everybody."

"Yeah—but I never wanted it to be hard on you."

David shrugged and looked down at the floor.

King took a deep breath. This wasn't exactly the meaningful rapprochement he'd hoped for. What had Peyton said? That they weren't communicating.

He backed up and tried again. "Son . . . for some reason you and I seem to be on different wavelengths lately."

David snorted. "Alert the media, why don't ya?"

"And I'd really like to get past the sarcasm."

"You've got the floor."

"Okay." King looked around and spotted a nearby stool. He sat on it and propped his elbow on his knee, then settled his chin on his fist. "I'm here and I'm listening. Talk to me, David. Tell me about this art school idea."

David's eyes narrowed. "Nothing to talk about, really. I'm going to CalArts. End of story."

"And you expect to earn your tuition by working *here*?"

"I expect to pay for my plane ticket working here. I'll figure out the rest when I get to L.A."

King sighed and rubbed the back of his neck. Deep breaths. He would not get upset; he would not yell. Those reactions never paid off, especially with young adults.

"Okay." He looked up again. "Would you mind telling me where all this interest is coming from? This recently discovered passion for art—it's news to me."

David's face seemed to soften as his eyes brightened with speculation. "It's not a sudden thing, Dad."

"No?"

"No. It's something I got interested in a while ago." He lowered his gaze, appearing to study his shoes. "After you and Mom split up, art was . . . kind of a distraction for me. From, you know, all the stuff that was going on between you two."

King folded one arm across his chest and rubbed his chin, carefully considering what he needed to say. What he should have said years ago.

"Those were really rough times," he began. "For all of us. But they were especially tough on you, I know. What I regret most about the whole awful mess was the chasm that opened up between us, and that I, to this day, haven't been able to bridge it. I could have done better. I *should* have done better. And for that failure, I am truly and profoundly sorry."

David stared at him, his face locked in neutral.

"Look, Son." King spread his hands. "If you want to go to California and draw pictures, that's fine by me. I'll support you in every way I can."

A slow smile inched across David's face. "Okay. Cool. But just so you know, it's not drawing I'm into."

The mental image of his son in a beret popped like a balloon. "No?"

"*This* is what I do." David gestured to the metal trays on the counter. King slipped off the stool and moved forward, looking at the prints clipped to a drying line. He threw a startled glance at David, then moved down the line and studied the dangling images of athletes in action, incredible shots of poetic grace, balance, and beauty. David had captured runners, wrestlers, gymnasts, Special Olympians . . . and baseball players, of course.

King couldn't pry his eyes away from the remarkable photos. "You shot these?"

"I know they're not all that good, but—"

"Not that good—are you kidding? These are amazing!"

He looked over in time to see a blush darken his son's cheeks. "Well, they were good enough to get me into CalArts, anyway. Someday, though, who knows? I mean, if you can win a Pulitzer, maybe it's in the genes. Maybe I can win one for photography."

King looked away, realizing with numb astonishment that for years the evidence of this talent had been right before his eyes. How many times had he seen David with a camera hanging from his neck? Whenever they visited a warehouse store, King headed for the golf equipment, but he usually found David among the cameras and lenses. At the time, he'd thought the kid simply liked to snap photos of his friends.

He turned and set his hands on his son's shoulders. "Somehow, David, somewhere along the way, I seem to have forgotten what an incredible kid you are. If you can forgive your old man for that, I promise . . . it'll never happen again."

Then, while David stammered in embarrassed pleasure, King drew his beloved son into his arms.

Twenty-one

KEENLY FEELING THE aftereffects of her long drive to Alexandria, on Thursday morning Peyton pulled herself out of bed, showered, and drove directly to Eve Miller's house. She had until 10:00 a.m. to talk to Eve; then she had to rush back to the office and write her Friday column. With that safely filed, she'd have the rest of the day, plus tomorrow, to finish the feature . . . and hope she could come up with something worth reading.

By the time she arrived at Eve's house, the newspaper was missing from the front lawn and the flag on the mailbox had been raised, a good indication that the lady of the house was awake and going about her business. Peyton knocked firmly and noted with relief that Eve didn't seem at all surprised to find a frustrated columnist on her front porch.

"You *are* an early bird," Eve remarked, her voice dry. "I was just reading the paper. Would you like to join me for a cup of tea?"

"I'd prefer coffee, if you have it," Peyton said, noticing that

Eve held a cup of something strong and aromatic. "I could use a heavy-duty dose of caffeine."

"I think we can arrange that. Follow me."

As Eve led the way through the studio and into a small kitchen, Peyton breathlessly spilled her story: how she'd gone to Alexandria, found Ben Morrick a widower, and offered him Eve's phone number. About how he'd handed the number back, insisting that the next move had to originate with Eve.

"But he wants to see you; I know it," Peyton finished, sliding into a chair. A pair of salt and pepper shakers stood at the center of the table, along with a framed photo of Eve's daughter. "I could see it in his eyes. He still cares for you, Evie."

One of Eve's arched brows shot up at Peyton's use of the familiar nickname. "Only Ben has ever called me by that name."

"Well, he still thinks of you that way. As King would say, the ball is now in your court . . . so what are you going to do about it?"

Eve stared at the folded newspaper on the table, shifting the focus of her gaze to some interior field of vision Peyton could only imagine. Silence ticked by.

Finally she turned to Peyton, her eyes hot and narrow. "Who gave you the right to do that? How could you take it upon yourself to go all the way up to Alexandria—"

Peyton blanched. "How could I *not* go? I'm working on an article and I needed information you weren't willing to give."

A warning cloud settled on Eve's features. "I never said you could use my personal life for your article. I thought we were having a conversation."

"A conversation, yes—another word for *interview*. You knew I was writing a story. Besides, you don't have to worry; I won't use your full name without your permission. I won't use any identifying details, though I don't see why it would matter if people read your story."

"You don't know everything about me. Really, you know very little."

Peyton laughed to cover her rising irritation. "I know you've made a case for passion because you were too cautious and lost the love of your life. Yet when I offer you a second chance at that love, what do you do? Accuse me of *meddling*?"

Eve shook her head. "You don't know the full story."

"Seems pretty cut-and-dried to me. You loved Ben; he loved you. You let him go, but now you're both free and you're both alone. What's to stop you from picking up where you left off?"

Eve rubbed her temple as if a headache had begun to pound there. "I would never have sent you that note if I'd thought you'd contact him. You don't understand the—"

"Good grief, Eve, *what* don't I understand? If I'm missing a piece of the puzzle, I wish you'd fill it in so I can see the full picture."

"I thought you'd figure it out, Ms. Heart Healer." Eve's stare drilled into her, the blue eyes blazing. "I can't see Ben because I stole something from him—something precious."

Peyton blinked. "He didn't mention anything like—"

"He didn't know. My daughter is *his* daughter. Not Billy's, Ben's."

For a moment Peyton could do nothing but stare at the photo

on the table; then the pieces clicked together. Dawn Miller—those brown eyes, that dimpled chin. Then and now, those features belonged to Ben Morrick.

She groaned. "I am so dense. I should have seen it."

"I won't argue that point." Eve stood and moved to the kitchen window. When she spoke again, her voice had gone soft with memory. "By the time I realized I was pregnant, Ben had shipped out. It was the autumn of 1966, an election year. My father, the judge, was running on a platform of what we'd now refer to as 'family values.'" She sighed and lowered her teacup into the sink. "I had no idea how Ben would take the news, but I was certain of my family's reaction."

Peyton folded her arms on the small table. "Let me guess—your wedding to Billy was right around the corner."

Eve exhaled softly. "The flowers had been ordered; the caterer engaged. Ben was gone. Billy had been assigned to a stateside post. So I chose caution over passion. Safety over love."

Peyton let the silence stretch; then she stood and moved to Eve's side. "That was forty years ago, Eve. Billy's gone. Your daughter's grown. What's stopping you from making things right?"

Eve gave her an incredulous look. "I stole Ben's child from him. Raised her with another man's name. How can he forgive that? After all these years, how would I begin to explain? Where would I find the words?"

Peyton slipped her arm around the older woman's shoulders. "In the same place I found words to tell my child I once tried to take her life along with my own. And failing that, I gave her away . . . because I didn't have the strength to be what she needed." She tapped the spot over her heart. "I found the words here, Eve. For years I begged God to help me find peace about what I'd done, and He answered my prayers by bringing my daughter back to me. When I found the courage to confess the truth, to my astonishment Christine responded, not with the disdain I'd expected, but with a flood of forgiveness and love."

Eve turned her head and eyed Peyton as if weighing her words. "It takes a lot of strength to overcome that kind of fear." Her soft voice held a note halfway between disbelief and sympathy. "Here you are, talking to me about faith and courage, yet you're not brave enough to commit your heart to your sports editor. Why is that, I wonder?"

Peyton drew in a quick breath, then released Eve's shoulder and gripped the edge of the kitchen counter as Eve's question stabbed at her heart. "I think it's because I—"

"Don't tell me," Eve interrupted softly. "Tell him."

With an hour before her column deadline, Peyton closed her eyes and hunched over her laptop, searching for the right words. She'd come home instead of driving to the newspaper office, knowing she needed profound quiet and solitude to write this most personal of columns.

Eve's challenge had rung in her ears all the way home, but the situation with King would have to wait until she could concentrate on him. At this moment, her heart was too bewildered by emotions, her head too full of words.

As for the feature on Eve Miller—maybe it had been a bad idea from the start. But the experience might give her enough fodder for the column due today . . . and if she wrote well, maybe this piece would help mend her tattered relationship with King.

She opened the file she'd labeled "EMiller.doc" and skimmed what she'd previously written. She highlighted and deleted the filler paragraphs about a columnist's job but kept the introductory material about Eve.

She scrolled to the end of the document and began to type:

. . . If you met Eve on the street, you'd notice her quick smile and honest blue eyes.

You'd also realize, by her clothing and personal style, that Eve is a woman with great passions. She's an artist, a decorator, and altogether unconventional. Yet more than four decades ago, my critic and new friend chose a well-marked path rather than risk an unblazed trail. Her regret at having made that choice has lasted a lifetime. And when, after all these years, fate offered a chance to choose a "do-over," if you will, Eve balked. Why? Because of a long-harbored secret . . . and fear.

Why has this otherwise brave woman been terrified into emotional paralysis? Because she's afraid this opportunity will prove to be an illusion. That she won't be welcomed with open arms.

But mostly, she's afraid she won't be forgiven.

I am familiar with all of those fears. I once longed

to reconcile with my father, whom I'd shut out, and my daughter, whom I'd abandoned. My fears imprisoned me in a dense and lonely darkness for years.

Then a stranger handed me a note—a simple note washed up from a plane crash, a few scribbled words on tattered paper. "I love you," the note said. "All is forgiven."

My attempt to deliver that note proved surprisingly difficult. For various reasons, people were reluctant to accept the message. And then I learned that the note was meant for my daughter . . . and me.

When I gathered up my slippery courage and stepped forward in the faith that I could be forgiven, I was . . . and what's more, I was received more joyfully than I deserved to be. But isn't that what love does?

I have tried to urge my friend Eve to step out in this same certainty, but deeply personal decisions often require preparation. We try to calm our pounding hearts. We load up on comfort foods. We fortify our souls with prayer and beg God to drop a brick on our heads if we're about to do the wrong thing.

But how could reconciliation be wrong when Christ came all the way to earth to make peace between God and fallen man?

Following His example, with open hands and hearts we should approach the ones we've wronged with humility, honesty, and gratitude. They may not love us as perfectly as God does, but if they love us at all, they will forgive.

Because that's what love does.

Peyton propped her elbow on the table and dropped her fore-head to her hand, then groaned as the truth of her own words hit home.

What was she doing? How could she write about Eve when she had not yet dealt with the broken relationships in her own life?

An hour ago she'd stood in Eve's kitchen and doled out advice she wasn't willing to take—and Eve had seen straight through her, of course. Peyton had always found it easier to preach a message than to live it; it was far easier to write about healing hearts than to set her own wounded heart on the operating table to undergo the painful experience of stitching it up. Healing meant exposure, the baring of secrets, and pain—oh, the pain!

But refusing to heal meant inflicting pain on someone else, someone who didn't deserve it.

She'd been wrong to shove the situation with King aside. She'd been wrong about a lot of things.

Love couldn't be defined by a debate over caution versus passion; both had their roles to play. Love was a daily exercise, a steadfast commitment to forgiving and sharing and listening.

Love . . . was what she'd seen in King, even as she kept him safely outside her heart.

Sighing, she pushed away from the dining room table and climbed the stairs. At the entrance to her bedroom, she paused in the doorway and looked at the framed picture on her dresser—a photograph of her and Gil in the backseat of the limo that drove them away from her wedding. In that frozen moment, she was laughing and holding on to her veil; Gil was grinning at some-one on the sidewalk.

She used to say that was the happiest day of her life . . . even though the marriage had ended in heartbreak.

She could no longer say that. She would no longer look back. Love had presented her with another chance to choose, and she would not forfeit it.

She stepped forward, lifted the wedding picture, and tucked it beneath the satiny fabrics in her lingerie drawer.

If she was going to move forward, it was time to put the past away.

Eve sat at her potter's wheel, her fingers lightly skimming the edge of the clay on the spinning circle. She'd been dreaming of this project for weeks—a series of four platters, each depicting a different season of a woman's life. She'd do the first one in shades of green, perhaps with childish lettering beneath the glaze to spell out the word *girl* or *baby doll*. The second platter would be glazed in shades of pink, depicting the years of courtship, young love, and blossoming femininity. She would paint a pair of lips at the center, or if that effect proved too obvious or tacky, perhaps she'd simply paint a heart.

She'd been thinking of doing the third platter in the golden colors of autumn—browns, oranges, and russets—but now she wondered if it might not be better to feature more golds than reds. Gold was a more hopeful color . . . and Peyton MacGruder had given her reason to hope.

She dipped her fingers in the bowl of water at her side and smoothed the spinning platter's edge. She had begun to think, though she'd never admit it to anyone, that writing the columnist had been a foolish idea. A voice inside her head kept insisting that perhaps she'd written because her wounded heart kept crying out for help, and who better to provide it than the woman who called herself the Heart Healer?

No, that was crazy. She'd written because Peyton didn't know what she was talking about . . . or maybe she knew all too well. Like Eve, Peyton lived in an emotional straitjacket, yet somehow she had the audacity to tell the world that living under such restraint was good, even desirable.

It wasn't. But surrendering to one's passions could result in serious consequences.

Eve snapped the button on the wheel's motor and waited until the spinning clay came to a complete stop. Then she used her knife to free the platter from the wheel and carried her creation to a shelf for air-drying.

When she stepped back, Peyton's words rushed back to her in a surge of memory: *"When I found the courage to confess the truth, to my astonishment Christine responded, not with the disdain I'd expected, but with a flood of forgiveness and love."*

Forgiveness and love—was such a result even possible? Could Ben offer love after Eve's defection and deception? Could Dawn's love remain unchanged if Eve confessed that the man she'd known as *Daddy* wasn't her father at all? that her conception had been the result of a reckless passion?

The pragmatic voice inside her head roared *no*, but Peyton had spoken with such conviction.

"When I found the courage to confess the truth . . ."

Eve had exhibited such courage once, on the railing of a bridge over a deep ravine. She had found courage in Ben's eyes, in his sure and steady grip.

Heaven help her find it there again.

After filing her column via e-mail, Peyton ate a quick lunch at home, brushed her teeth, and drove to the newspaper office. Nora would be waiting, probably with a list of suggestions about the piece, but who could predict how she'd react? Maybe she'd like what she read.

If she wanted to suggest revisions, though, she'd have to wait. Peyton had a more pressing errand to complete, one that would not be postponed. Her talk with Eve this morning had convinced her of one thing: she had to find King and come clean about why she'd been so reluctant to accept his proposal. She had to pray he'd understand.

She took the stairs instead of the elevator, pasting a smile on her face in case she encountered him in his favorite hideaway. She turned the corner that led to the newsroom and felt her smile fade. King wasn't on the stairs.

Okay, then. He must be working in his office like a proper professional. She strengthened her resolve and opened the door. She was halfway to the editorial offices when a high voice halted her in midstride.

"Peyton! You made it in."

She turned and saw Mandi emerging from a cubicle, a stack of printouts in her arms.

"I always do, eventually." She jerked her thumb toward King's office. "Is His Majesty around?"

"I haven't seen him, but I haven't been around much today. Been hiding out in the library."

Peyton lifted a brow. "Hiding from whom?"

"Nora—she called three times before I had my first latte. First she wanted to know how you're coming on that feature; then she wanted me to remind you that she was waiting on your column."

Peyton groaned. "I've scrapped the feature I had in mind. But she has the column now; I e-mailed it with five minutes to spare."

Mandi's face fell. "So—after all my hard work, you're not going to write about Eve Miller?"

"I wrote about her today. But don't be disappointed—I might want to do a follow-up."

"That explains Nora's third call. She has a list of queries."

"I'll give her a call . . . later. Right now I need to see someone."

Peyton walked to King's office and knocked on the closed door. No answer. She tried the doorknob, fully expecting it to be locked, but the door swung open. In the space beyond, King's chair, desk, and bookcases had been covered with drop cloths. A painter on a ladder glanced over his shoulder. "Can I help you?"

"Um . . ." Peyton's gaze darted frantically as panic rose from the marrow of her bones. King's books, his trophies, the plaques that had hung on his wall—someone had dropped everything into boxes and shoved them toward the door. "No." Her voice sounded strangled. "I don't think so."

She closed the door and walked back to the table where Mandi was collating copies. "Are you sure you haven't seen—" She groaned as a sudden thought struck. If King wasn't in his office or in his secret hideout, where could he be?

New York. The *Times*.

She swallowed the heart that had risen into her throat. Reason told her to remain calm, to postpone this conversation and go talk to Nora, but passion urged her to drop everything and find King before she lost him forever.

Peyton inhaled deeply as a cold coil of certainty tightened in her chest. Wouldn't Eve Miller love to see her now? Eve would shake her well-groomed head, cluck her tongue, and say, "I told you so. You cannot live your entire life under cautious restraint."

Well, okay, Eve. You were right about that, but I'm not finished living yet.

"Mandi—" she reached for the girl's arm—"you know that direct flight from Middleborough to JFK? What time does it leave?"

Mandi glanced at the clock high on the wall. "About an hour ago."

Peyton made a noise that sounded like all the vowels run together, then raked her hand through her hair. "This isn't working."

"What's not working?" Mandi's anxious eyes searched Peyton's face. "You okay?"

Struggling against tears she refused to let fall, Peyton stared at the clock. Though she had work to do, though she had obligations, and though she hadn't given a moment's thought as to what came next, she wasn't about to give up. She loved King Danville and she was going after him. Running off to Manhattan might be impulsive, it might be *crazy*, but sometimes you couldn't take a chance on waiting.

She tightened her grip on Mandi's arm. "I need you to book a seat for me on the next flight to LaGuardia or JFK. Never mind about connections; I'll take whatever's going to New York. You can text me with the flight info. I'm going home to pack a bag."

She released the intern and strode toward the elevator.

"Wait! What about Nora's queries?" Mandi panted, struggling to keep up.

"Stall her."

"Me?"

"Who else?"

"How?"

"Don't know. Don't care." Peyton stepped into the elevator and blew the startled intern a farewell kiss. "I'm following my heart."

Twenty-two

FLUSHED FROM THE warmth of the afternoon sun, Ben Morrick snipped a couple of parrot tulips near the base of their stems, then moved down the flower bed to cut a hyacinth stalk. A bee buzzed around the brilliant blossoms, so Ben waited until it had flown away before he made the cut. The wind shifted, blowing the thick, sweet scent of the hyacinths over his face. These flowers would perfume his entire kitchen.

He startled as his garden gate creaked on its hinges. He turned, swiveling on his knees, and saw a tall, slim woman backlit against the blinding afternoon sun.

"Hello, Ben."

Even across the span of forty years, he would know that voice anywhere.

After lowering the thermostat and refilling the cats' bowls, Peyton picked up her overnight bag and hurried toward the door. A

PanWorld flight would be departing in less than two hours, so if she hurried she could be in New York by dinnertime.

She opened the front door and stared at King, whose hand had frozen as if he was preparing to ring the bell.

She blinked. "You're here."

He glanced down at her suitcase. "Where you're obviously not planning to stay. Where are you off to in such a hurry?"

She stared, wondering if she should pinch herself. "I'm booked on a flight to New York. I thought you'd accepted the—"

He shook his head, a smile tugging at the corners of his mouth.

"But . . . they're painting your office. They've cleaned everything out. Your stuff is in boxes; I saw them."

"You don't think I'd leave my awards out to get paint dripped on them, do you?" He grinned. "The paint job is part of the deal I made with Nora to keep me from going to the *Times*. Of course, I didn't tell her I had far more pressing reasons to stay in Middleborough."

Peyton's breath caught in her lungs. "You . . . you turned down the job?"

"You're surprised?"

She gaped at him and lowered her suitcase to the floor. "Before you tell me why, King, there's something I need to tell you."

He sucked at the inside of his cheek for a minute, then nodded. "Okay."

"Come on in." She led him into the house, shoving her overnight bag out of the way as they moved through the foyer. In the living room, she took a moment to sort through her thoughts, then whirled to face him. "I've been thinking about what to say all afternoon and practicing for an hour. But I still might mess things up."

He slipped his hands into his pockets. "Take your time, MacGruder. I'll wait."

"Good." She drew another deep breath. "You were right, you know. About me using Christine as an excuse to not commit to you. To us."

King didn't answer but sank to the edge of the sofa and studied her face with considerable concentration.

"The truth was—the truth *is*—that I was afraid. I was—I *am*—terrified that we'll get married, and then one day you'll wake up and realize that I'm not good enough for you. I know you think you love me now, but I'm not that special, King, and one day you're going to realize it—"

"Hang on a minute." He frowned at her like a man faced with a difficult problem in trigonometry. "I'll never understand why you can't seem to realize just how wonderful you are." He started to stand, as if to embrace her, but Peyton warded him off with an uplifted hand.

"There's more," she continued, her voice breaking. "I've told you about Gil. How we met. He was the cool professor, me the adoring student. Our relationship was built on passion mostly, and I was young and naive enough to believe it would last."

Surprise flickered across his face. "It didn't?"

"When I got pregnant, Gil became . . . distant. He found reasons not to spend time at home. I began to suspect an affair."

King's brows flickered. "I didn't realize. I thought you two were soul mates—"

"And desperately in love, right? I know, it's what I wanted people to believe. I didn't want anyone to know the truth." She hesitated as images from the painful past flooded her mind. "I confronted Gil the night of his accident. Accused him of betraying our marriage. He denied it, of course. We screamed at one another, said vile things I'll never forget. Then he walked out into the rain . . . and I never saw him alive again."

Lines of concentration deepened under King's eyes. "Was it true? What you suspected?"

Peyton blinked back a sudden rush of tears. "Several days after I buried him, a letter arrived at the house. One of his grad students wrote to say that we'd met once, but I didn't remember her. She was looking . . . for absolution, I suppose, because she told me she'd had an affair with my husband."

A small flicker of shock widened his eyes. "I'm sorry," King whispered.

"She said Gil had gone to her place and ended it that night. He was driving home to beg my forgiveness when he slid off the road and hit the tree."

King rose from the sofa and pulled Peyton into his arms. She melted in his embrace, but she hadn't finished; he deserved to know the entire truth.

"That's when I stopped trusting my heart," she whispered, grateful that he hadn't given up when confronted with her stubbornness. "Because even if it was true and Gil was coming home to confess, I knew him well enough to know he might stray again.

I wasn't enough woman for him, you see? So I was afraid the passion you feel for me would disappear like it had with Gil and I'd be left with nothing but guilt and grief and anger. I couldn't face that again, no matter how much I love you. But now . . ."

"What changed?" His eyes glittered with curiosity.

"Having met another woman who squandered a lifetime of love because of misguided fear, I realized I couldn't let that happen to me. To us." She hiccuped a sob and dashed a tear from her cheek. "I may not be the greatest prize in the world, but if you want me, King, I'm yours."

"Peyton." He pressed his lips to her cheek, his breath a warm whisper on her skin. "If Gil were with us now, I'd be tempted to work him over for what he did to you. He did wrong, Peyton, to make you feel like anything less than the most precious woman in the world. Because that's what you are—warm, wonderful, insightful, and—" he chuckled—"sometimes even witty."

She sniffed and managed a trembling smile. "I can't cook."

"Who cares?" Smiling, he lowered his forehead to hers. "The world is full of interesting restaurants."

"I'm also insecure, I rush around a lot, and sometimes I write in bed."

Amusement sparked in his eyes. "I know you, Peyton, and I love you. And if you want to write in bed, I'll join you. Maybe I'll start on my memoirs."

She laughed, relaxing in his arms, then tipped her head back to look up at him. "So tell me—why did you turn down that job in New York?"

His expression remained serious, but one corner of his mouth curled upward. "Had to. I found myself sitting in the *Times* conference room fantasizing about your panty hose drying on my shower curtain."

She laughed. "What?"

"Weird, huh? I know. I kept imagining my last razor blade being used to shave your gorgeous legs. Couldn't stop thinking about how little closet space I actually need . . . but how much I *do* need you, Peyton MacGruder."

She laughed again as he released her and stepped toward her favorite chair. "Couldn't imagine going to sleep at night—" he picked up a decorative pillow—"without imagining your feet entwined with mine. Couldn't write a lick without missing your wonderfully distracting kisses. Couldn't conceive of a future without you in it."

"Such a great opportunity for you," Peyton whispered, her heart hammering. "The Gray Lady. You, hobnobbing with the big shots in Manhattan. I can't believe you gave it up for me."

"I already have all I want—" his fingers stroked her cheek— "right here."

King smiled into her eyes, dropped the pillow at her feet, and knelt on one knee, joints snapping as he groaned and lowered himself to the floor. He pulled a familiar square box from his pocket and lifted her hand. "If you don't want this today, Peyton, that's okay. Because I intend to propose to you every day for as long as it takes for you to feel you're ready to say—"

"Yes," she interrupted.

He lifted his brows. "Yes? As in yes, you want me to propose every day, or yes, you'll marry me?"

"Both." She thought she might burst from the sudden swell of happiness that flooded her heart. She looked down and smiled, then lowered herself to his level, kissing him so thoroughly he could have no doubts at all.

Ben stared at the woman sitting beside him, amazed and almost afraid to believe Eve had actually come. But there she was, as lovely and vibrant as on the day they had parted. He had felt the softness of her skin when he took her hand; he heard the delicate tones of her voice when she greeted him. And though their bodies had grown softer and their hands had freckled, Eve's blue eyes had not changed. They were the same—wide, clever, and sparkling.

Sitting in a pair of Adirondack chairs in his garden, they talked for half an hour about trivial things—the weather, their homes, their careers. He told her about his marriage to Linh, the quiet and devoted woman he had met in Vietnam. His marriage had not been as intense as his relationship with Eve, but he had not been alone in the passing years. They had no children, but he and Linh had loved each other until the day she died.

And then, just as Ben knew it would, the conversation turned to the last day he and Eve had seen each other.

"After that day in the rain," Eve said, one hand smoothing out her skirt, "I was confused. About who I was and who I wanted to be. I felt guilty, of course, about what I—what *we'd*—done. It took a while for me to sort it all out. To realize that my love for you was real . . . even though I hadn't chosen the best way to express it. But by the time I rode to the base to tell you what I had—"

He felt a curious, tingling shock. "You rode over? On your bike?"

She laughed softly. "How else? I didn't bother to slow down at the guard gate. Got arrested by the MPs for my trouble." Her smile faded. "But not before I made it to your quarters and found that you'd left that morning. You were on your way to Vietnam, and I was left . . . without you."

Ben shook his head. "I can't believe I missed you by a few hours. If only . . ."

"What? What would we have done? run off? gotten married?"

"Maybe. Why not?"

She tilted her head and gave him a wistful smile. "What different lives we would have led."

"But why didn't you write? or call?"

"I would have—" her smile vanished—"but the next day, I found out I was pregnant."

He gripped the armrest of his chair as the colors of the garden blurred and whirled around him. *Pregnant?*

"You were gone, Ben, to the other side of the world, and I didn't know if you were coming back. Frankly, given your penchant for risk taking, I didn't think you would. I tortured myself for days; then I turned in the only direction I could. To the world I knew best."

"To Billy, you mean." The words came out gruffer than he intended.

Tears welled in her lovely eyes. "I decided the best thing under the circumstances was to avoid a scandal and protect our families' reputations. So I went through with the wedding. The baby was born eight months later."

Ben stared at Eve, struggling to make sense of her confession. She'd been pregnant. With his child. Surely it was true, or she wouldn't be weeping.

He stood and walked toward the picket fence, keeping his back to her as he pretended a sudden fascination for the parrot tulips. A sea of emotion churned within him, and he wasn't sure he could trust the expressions on his face. He didn't want to hurt Eve—she looked profoundly vulnerable around the eyes—but he couldn't stop a surge of resentment from coloring his thoughts.

How many times had he comforted Linh when she failed to become pregnant? How many nights had he knelt and begged God to bless them with a child? Yet all the while he had one . . . who thought she belonged to someone else.

"Marrying Billy was a cowardly decision I regretted even as I stood before the pastor," Eve continued, her words coming faster now. "Because you were always there, Ben, between Billy and me. After he died, I tried to find you. Dawn was only four then, so I had this fantasy of finding you and putting things to rights, the way they should have been. But after Richie told me you were married, I did everything I could to put you out of my mind, even though I failed miserably."

Ben thrust his hands into his pockets and shivered as a sough of wind set a bare branch of a dogwood to tapping against the fence.

"I don't blame you for feeling angry or betrayed." Eve's voice dissolved into a thready whisper. "I would understand if you never wanted to see me again. When Peyton MacGruder found you, I wanted to stay away because I didn't think I could summon up enough courage to tell you the truth."

He turned and met her steadfast gaze. In the line of her jaw he saw determination, but she had always been brave. The years of uncertainty had cost her, though, for lines of suffering were faintly etched around her eyes and mouth.

"Yet here you are," he said simply.

She nodded, her cheeks coloring under the heat of his gaze. "Yes."

Somehow his past had looped around and connected to his present, joining an old passion and a present mystery. Eve Jackson Miller was sitting in his garden, gilded by the afternoon sun, her hair, lighter now, ruffled by the rising breeze. The years had marked her, as they had him, but surely the passing time had also granted them a store of wisdom. They were talking openly, no longer worried about prior claims, parents, or superior officers.

Somewhere another war was raging, but Ben would let younger men fight this one. He had earned a rest. Perhaps Eve had, too.

In that instant, he forgave her. Together they had fallen in love, and together they had made a mistake. But until now Eve had been suffering the consequences alone, and she didn't deserve that.

He had betrayed Billy, too.

"I'm glad you've come." He turned and sat in the chair beside her, pulling her chilly hands from her lap. "I want you to tell me everything. Everything about your life that I've missed."

Tears sparkled now above her tremulous smile. "There's so much, I hardly know where to start."

He lifted her hand, kissed the tips of her fingers, and looked into her eyes. "We have time. You can begin by telling me about our baby."

She laughed, and the sound of her joy filled the garden. "We have a beautiful daughter, Ben. Her name is Dawn."

"Dawn?" How appropriate. This felt like the birth of a new day.

"And I don't want to make you feel old," she went on, "but you also have grandchildren. Not just one, but two boys . . . who look very much like you."

He accepted the news in wonder, then tipped back his head, freeing a laugh to ripple on the air.

Twenty-three

PEYTON AND CHRISTINE sat on a stone wall overlooking the ocean while Peyton struggled to catch her breath. They'd run at least two miles, and Peyton had insisted that they take a break before turning around and heading back to the car. Though she was far from being as winded as her mother, Christine had agreed.

The wind blew in from the sea with the promise of summer in its breath, the warm hope of good things to come. The setting sun painted the ocean with tints of crimson and tangerine.

Peyton leaned back on her hands and exhaled a long sigh of contentment.

"So, you did it." Christine playfully elbowed Peyton's ribs. "You finally said you'd marry him?"

Peyton nodded. "You gonna be okay with that?"

"I'm going to be great. I like King a lot. I even like the idea of gaining a brother."

Surprised at the depth of her relief, Peyton slipped an arm

around Christine's shoulders. "I haven't asked you the most important question: will you be my maid of honor?"

Christine pressed her hand to her chest in pretend amazement. "Me?"

"Who else?"

"I'd be honored." Christine lowered her hand and looked at Peyton, her eyes softening with seriousness. "It means a lot that you'd ask."

"And I promise—no ugly dresses. You can wear whatever you'd like." Peyton squeezed her shoulder. "David's going to be King's best man. Mandi keeps hinting that she wants to do something at the wedding, so I think I'll let her handle the guest book. Or maybe the punch bowl."

"Speaking of Mandi—" Christine arched a brow—"did you ever finish that big article your editor wanted? You know, that special thing the syndicate wanted to see?"

"The anniversary feature." Peyton nodded. "Wrote it this morning; handed it in with time to spare. After last night, the words just sort of flowed out of me."

Christine shook her head. "Remind me to call you the next time I need to write a term paper. I need you to teach me that trick."

"It's not a trick." Peyton's voice went soft. "Either the words and the feelings are inside you, or they're not."

They sat in companionable silence until a broad-winged gull rose up from the waves and took flight.

"Mom?"

Peyton felt a thrill shiver through her senses. Christine didn't use the word *Mom* often, but she was beginning to say it more frequently. "Yeah?"

"Thank you."

"For what?"

One of Christine's shoulders moved upward in a shrug as the wind blew a curtain of hair across her face. "For choosing to love me. For coming into my life—and staying in it—when you didn't have to."

Peyton reached out and tenderly pulled a windblown strand from Christine's porcelain cheek, entranced, once again, by the miracle that had brought them back together. "Sweetheart, I wouldn't have missed you for the world."

The Heart Healer, Anniversary Edition

The Middleborough Times *would like to congratulate Peyton MacGruder for a successful first year as the Heart Healer.*

Dear Readers:

Those of you who have been faithful readers over the past year have traveled with me through several interesting life challenges. I'll be the first to admit I'm often a slow learner, but I have picked up a few lessons along the way. You, my readers, have often been my best teachers.

Many of you sent me stories of your "crossroads experiences" and other assorted adventures. Thank you for your help. Reading through them has helped me realize that I'm not alone on life's journey. None of us are. Your willingness to share and respond has sharpened me at times and softened me at others. You have made me laugh and cry. Most of all, you have made me think.

As I've shared my heart with you, I have learned that

the entire spectrum of human emotion is open to us all. Though our experiences are vastly different, our feelings are very much the same. My happiness is virtually identical to yours; your grief could be a twin to mine. Because the heart responds with the same feelings, I'm often able to give advice that helps everyone . . . everyone willing to heed it, that is.

One of my readers recently reminded me that I have a tendency to dispense good medicine, though I'm not always willing to swallow it myself. So I have decided to take my own advice and proceed boldly through the crossroads of indecision and into a new life chapter.

Why? In part because our children, no matter what their ages, learn their most powerful lessons from what they see in us; their lessons are more caught than taught.

I have recently been offered a chance to share love again. And if I passed it up because I'm afraid I might suffer loss or pain, I'd be setting the wrong example for my daughter. More than that, I'd be denying myself the opportunity to love the most wonderful man in the world, who by some miracle loves me, too.

I have lived in the prison of fear and doubt; I have let those chains bind my dreams for far too long. I have learned that Sophocles was right: to him who lives in fear, everything rustles.

I don't want my daughter to be afraid of life. I want my darling girl to believe in love. I want her to be delighted by a romance. I want her to observe the way a man treasures the woman he loves. I want her to realize that a cherished woman does not surrender her personhood in a marriage relationship but rather grows stronger and more confident because she is loved. I want her to know that the source of love is God, who told us fear has no place in love.

I have a friend who recently reconnected with an old love, but she had to overcome her own fears to take those brave steps. She tells me they are now experiencing the adventure of becoming reacquainted after several years and two separate lifetimes. My friend is renewing what she feared was a passion long lost.

I wish her all the happiness her heart can hold.

As for me, I'll be on a honeymoon hiatus next week. But I'd like to leave you with something to ponder during your coffee break: Love is alive and constantly evolving. Don't attempt to understand it, reason with it, or defer it. Most of all, don't deny it entry into your heart. Banish your doubts and insecurities, and hold on to love for all you're worth.

Never let fear keep you from reaching for life's bouquets.

And never, ever, fail to take a chance on love.

About the Author

CHRISTY AWARD WINNER Angela Hunt writes books for readers who have learned to expect the unexpected. With over three million copies of her books sold worldwide, she is the best-selling author of *The Tale of Three Trees*, *The Note*, *Magdalene*, and more than 100 other titles.

She and her youth pastor husband make their home in Florida with mastiffs. One of their dogs was featured on *Live with Regis and Kelly* as the second-largest canine in America.

Readers may visit her Web site at www.angelahuntbooks.com.

Discussion Questions

1. John wrote, "God is love, and all who live in love live in God, and God lives in them. And as we live in God, our love grows more perfect. So we will not be afraid on the day of judgment, but we can face him with confidence because we live like Jesus here in this world. Such love has no fear, because perfect love expels all fear" (1 John 4:16-18).

   How does this passage, which refers to our love for God, translate into our love relationships with each other? How did fear prevent Peyton from fully trusting and completely loving King? How did fear come between Ben and Eve? What must happen before fear can be expelled?

2. "Man is only truly great when he acts from the passions."
   —Benjamin Disraeli
   "Serving one's own passions is the greatest slavery."
   —Thomas Fuller
   How are both of these opinions true? How can they both be true if they seem to contradict each other?

3. Eve disagreed with Peyton's statement that "caution should trump passion." At the beginning of the story, did you side with Eve or Peyton? Did you change your position as the story progressed?

4. If you were a newspaper columnist, what would be your greatest challenge? What is Peyton's greatest difficulty? What are her strengths?

5. If you've seen the movie or read the novel *The Note*, how has Peyton changed in the time between that story and this one?

6. Do you agree with Peyton's decision to tell Christine that she is the girl's biological mother?

7. Do you think King will break Peyton's heart like Gil did? Why or why not?

8. Is there a character in the novel with whom you identify? What is it about this person that strikes you as familiar?

9. One of Peyton's chief weaknesses is fear. In *The Note*, she experienced panic attacks. She seems to have those under control in this story, but anxiety still causes trouble for her. Do you fear? If so, what are you afraid of?

10. In Psalm 27, David wrote, "The Lord is my light and my salvation—so why should I be afraid? The Lord is my fortress, protecting me from danger, so why should I tremble?"

    What practical help can we discover in this verse when we feel ourselves becoming anxious and afraid? Is there anything on earth that can truly harm us?

11. What can you gain from a novel that you can't find in a film? What advantages does film hold over the printed page?

Author's Note

READERS WHO ARE familiar with my book *The Note* may notice a few differences between that book and this sequel. (I'm explaining this now so you won't have to write me later.) The reason for the differences is simple: *Taking a Chance on Love* is actually a sequel to the movie version of *The Note*, in which certain details from my book were changed. As a novelist, I had no choice but to contradict either the movie or the first novel. Fortunately, those details are minor and do not affect the plot or deep characterization. The characters remain unchanged—except that Lila, Peyton's daughter in *The Note* the novel, is now Christine, and a few other names have been changed. Like me, you may wonder why names change in the transfer process from page to film. The producers explained that this is due to a legal process whereby they must ensure the fictitious nature of the characters.

Another significant difference is the location. *The Note* the novel is set in Tampa Bay, my home, but the setting for *The Note* the movie was the fictional Middleborough, North Carolina.

Taking a Chance on Love is also set in Middleborough. Why that change? In another behind-the-scenes explanation, the producers shared that this decision was based on economics and the need to keep to a very tight production schedule. Most of the filming occurred in Toronto. North Carolina proved to be a location that matched both the geographical requirements for the story and the budget and time-frame needs. Its coastal landscapes are crucial to this story.

If you've seen the movie *Taking a Chance on Love*, you may notice a few additional minor differences between the film and this novelization. These are due to my enjoying the opportunity to enlarge the story world, escape film's time constraints, and delve a little deeper into the character's personalities. I had more freedom to depict the environment and job details of a working newspaper columnist.

I hope that the few differences will enhance your enjoyment of the story.

Blessings to you and yours!

Angela Hunt
www.angelahuntbooks.com

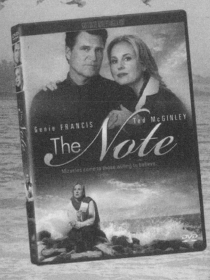
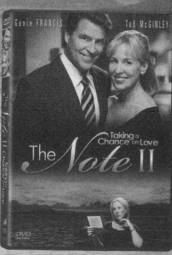

Other Novels by

Angela Hunt

Contemporary

Doesn't She Look Natural?   *The Truth Teller*

She Always Wore Red   *The Awakening*

She's in a Better Place   *The Debt*

The Face   *The Canopy*

Uncharted   *The Pearl*

The Elevator   *The Justice*

The Novelist   *The Note*

A Time to Mend   *The Immortal*

Unspoken

Historical

The Nativity Story   *The Velvet Shadow*

Magdalene   *The Emerald Isle*

The Shadow Women   *Dreamers*

The Silver Sword   *Brothers*

The Golden Cross   *Journey*

**For a complete listing,
visit www.angelahuntbooks.com**

CP0158

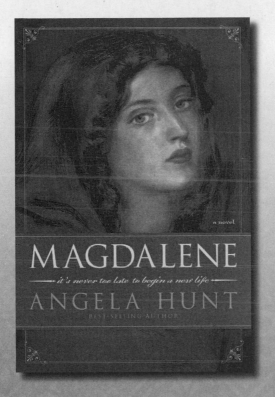

The Nativity Story—A novelization of the major motion picture. Best-selling author Angela Hunt presents a heartwarming adaptation of *The Nativity Story*. Hunt brings the story of Christ's birth to life with remarkable attention to detail and a painstaking commitment to historical accuracy.

Also available in Spanish.